What Katy Did

SUSAN M. COOLIDGE

What Katy Did

PARRAGON

What Katy Did
A Parragon Classic

This edition published in 1993 by
Parragon Book Service Ltd
Avonbridge Industrial Estate
Atlantic Road, Avonmouth
Bristol BS11 9QD

Printed and bound in Great Britain by
BPCC Paperbacks Ltd
Member of BPCC Ltd

CHAPTER ONE

THE LITTLE CARRS

I was sitting in the meadows one day, not long ago, at a place where there was a small brook. It was a hot day. The sky was very blue, and white clouds, like great swans, went floating over it to and fro. Just opposite me was a clump of green rushes, with dark velvety spikes, and among them one single tall, red cardinal flower, which was bending over the brook as if to see its own beautiful face in the water. But the cardinal did not seem to be vain.

The picture was so pretty that I sat a long time enjoying it. Suddenly, close to me, two small voices began to talk—or to sing, for I couldn't tell exactly which it was. One voice was shrill;-the other, which was a little deeper, sounded very positive and cross. They were evidently disputing about something, for they said the same words over and over again. These were the words—"Katy did." "Katy didn't." "She did." "She didn't." "She did." "She didn't." "Did." "Didn't." I think they must have repeated them at least a hundred times.

I got up from my seat to see if I could find the speakers; and sure enough, there on one of the cat-tail bulrushes, I spied two tiny pale green creatures. Their eyes seemed to be weak, for they both wore black goggles. They had six legs apiece—two short ones, two not so short, and two very long. These last legs had joints like the springs of a carriage; and as I watched, they began walking up the rush, and then I saw that they moved exactly like an old-fashioned gig. In fact, if I hadn't been too big, I *think* I should have heard them creak as they went along. They didn't say anything so long as I was there, but the moment my back was turned they began to quarrel again, and in the same old words—"Katy did." "Katy didn't." "She did." "She didn't."

As I walked home I fell to thinking about another Katy—a Katy I once knew, who planned to do a great many wonderful things, and in the end did none of them, but something quite different—something she didn't like at all at first, but which, on the whole, was a great deal better than any of the doings she had dreamed about. And as I thought, this little story grew in my head, and I resolved to write it down for you. I have done it; and, in memory of my two little friends on the bulrush, I give it their name. Here it is—the story of What Katy Did:

Katy's name was Katy Carr She lived in the town of Burnet, which wasn't a very big town, but was growing fast. The house she lived in stood on the edge of the town. It was a large square house, white, with green blinds, and had a porch in front, over which roses and clematis made a thick bower. Four tall locust trees shaded the gravel path which led to the front gate. On one side of the house was an orchard; on the other side were wood piles and barns, and an ice-house. Behind was a kitchen garden sloping to the south; and behind that a pasture with a brook in it, and butternut trees, and four cows—two red ones, a yellow one with sharp horns tipped with tin, and a dear little white one named Daisy.

There were six of the Carr children—four girls and two boys. Katy, the oldest, was twelve years old; little

Phil, the youngest, was four, and the rest fitted in between.

Dr. Carr, their papa, was a dear, kind, busy man, who was away from home all day, and sometimes all night, too, taking care of sick people. The children hadn't any mamma. She had died when Phil was a baby, four years before my story began. Katy could remember her pretty well; to the rest she was but a sad, sweet name, spoken on Sunday, and at prayer times, or when Papa was specially gentle and solemn.

In place of this mamma, whom they recollected so dimly, there was Aunt Izzie, Papa's sister, who came to take care of them when Mamma went away on that long journey, from which, for so many months, the little ones kept hoping she might return. Aunt Izzie was a small woman, sharp-faced and thin, rather old-looking, and very neat and particular about everything. She meant to be kind to the children, but they puzzled her much, because they were not a bit like herself when she was a child. Aunt Izzie had been a gentle, tidy little thing, who loved to sit as Curly Locks did, sewing long seams in the parlour, and to have her head patted by older people, and be told that she was a good girl; whereas Katy tore her dress every day, hated sewing, and didn't care a button about being called "good", while Clover and Elsie shied off like restless ponies when anyone tried to pat their heads. It was very perplexing to Aunt Izzie, and she found it hard to quite forgive the children for being so "strange", and so little like the good boys and girls in Sunday-school memoirs, who were the young people she liked best, and understood most about.

Then Dr. Carr was another person who worried her. He wished to have the children hardy and bold, and encouraged climbing and rough-plays, in spite of the bumps and ragged clothes which resulted. In fact, there was just one half-hour of the day when Aunt Lizzie was really satisfied about her charges, and that was the half-hour before breakfast, when she had made a law that they were all to sit in their little chairs and learn the Bible verse for the day. At this time she looked at them with pleased eyes; they were all so spick and span, with such nicely brushed jackets and such neatly combed hair. But the moment the bell rang her comfort was over. From that time on, they were what she called "not fit to be seen." The neighbours pitied her very much. They used to count the sixty stiff white pantalette legs hung out to dry every Monday morning, and say to each other what a sight of washing those children made, and what a trouble it must be for poor Miss Carr to keep them so nice. But poor Miss Carr didn't think them at all nice—that was the worst of it.

"Clover, go upstairs and wash your hands! Dorry, pick your hat off the floor and hang it on the nail! Not that nail— the third nail from the corner!" These were the kind of things Aunt Izzie was saying all day long. The children minded her pretty well, but they didn't exactly love her, I fear. They called her "Aunt Izzie" always, never "Aunty". Boys and girls will know what *that* meant. I want to show you the little Carrs, and I don't know that I could ever have a better chance than one day when five out-of the six were perched on top of the ice-house, like chickens on a roost. This ice-house was one of their favourite places. It was only a low roof set over a hole in the ground? and, as it stood in the middle of the side-yard, it always seemed to the children that the shortest road to every place was up one of its slopes and down the other. They also liked to mount to the ridgepole, and then, still keeping the sitting position, to let go, and scrape slowly down over

8

the warm shingles to the ground. It was bad for their shoes and trousers, of course, but what of that? Shoes and trousers, and clothes generally, were Aunt Izzie's affair; theirs was to slide and enjoy themselves.

Clover, next in age to Katy, sat in the middle. She was a fair, sweet dumpling of a girl, with thick pigtails of light brown hair, and short-sighted blue eyes, which seemed to hold tears, just ready to fall from under the blue. Really, Clover was the jolliest little thing in the world; but these eyes, and her soft cooing voice, always made people feel like petting her and taking her part. Once, when she was very small, she ran away with Katy' doll, and when Katy pursued, and tried to take it from her, Clover held fast and would not let go. Dr. Carr, who wasn't attending particularly, heard nothing but the pathetic tone of Clover's voice, as she said, "Me won't! Me want dolly," and, without stopping to inquire, he called out sharply, "For shame, Katy! give your sister *her* doll at once!", which Katy, much surprised, did; while Clover purred in triumph, like a satisfied kitten. Clover was sunny and sweet-tempered, a little indolent, and very modest about herself, though in fact she was particularly clever in all sorts of games, and extremely droll and funny in a quiet way. Everybody loved her, and she loved everybody, especially Katy, whom she looked up to as one of the wisest people in the world.

Pretty little Phil sat next on the roof to Clover, and she held him tight with her arm. Then came Elsie, a thin, brown child of eight, with beautiful dark eyes, and crisp, short curls covering the whole of her small head. Poor little Elsie was the "odd one" among the Carrs. She didn't seem to belong exactly to either the older or the younger children. The great desire and ambition of her heart was to be allowed to go about

9

with Katy and Clover and Cecy Hall, and to know their secrets, and be permitted to put notes into the little post offices they were for ever establishing in all sorts of hidden places. But they didn't want Elsie, and used to tell her to "run away and play with the children," which hurt her feelings very much. When she wouldn't run away, I am sorry to say they ran away from her, which, as their legs were longest, it was easy to do. Poor Elsie, left behind, would cry bitter tears, and, as she was too proud to play much with Dorry and John, her principal comfort was tracking the older ones about and discovering their mysteries, especially the post offices, which were her greatest grievance. Her eyes were bright and quick as a bird's. She would peep and peer, and follow and watch, till at last, in some odd, unlikely place—the crotch of a tree, the middle of the asparagus bed, or perhaps on the very top step of the scuttle ladder—she spied the little paper box, with its load of notes, all ending with "Be sure and not let Elsie know." Then she would seize the box, and, marching up to wherever the others were, she would throw it down, saying, defiantly, "There's your old post office!" but feeling all the time just like crying. Poor little Elsie! In almost every big family there is one of these unmated, left-out children. Katy, who had the finest plans in the world for being "heroic", and of use, never saw, as she drifted on her heedless way, that here, in this lonely little sister, was the very chance she wanted for being a comfort to somebody who needed comfort very much. She never saw it, and Elsie's heavy heart went uncheered.

Dorry and Joanna sat on the two ends of the ridge-pole. Dorry was six years old: a pale, pudgy boy, with rather a solemn face, and smears of molasses on the sleeve of his jacket. Joanna, whom the children called

"John" and "Johnnie", was a square, splendid child, a year younger than Dorry; she had big brave eyes and a wide rosy mouth, which always looked ready to laugh. These two were great friends, though Dorry seemed like a girl who had got into boy's clothes by mistake, and Johnnie like a boy who, in a fit of fun, had borrowed his sister's frock. And now, as they all sat there chattering and giggling, the window above opened, a glad shriek was heard, and Katy's head appeared. In her hand she held a heap of stockings, which she waved triumphantly.

"Hurray" she cried, "all done, and Aunt Izzie says we may go. Are you tired out waiting? I couldn't help it, the holes were *so* big, and took so long. Hurry up, Clover, and get the things! Cecy and I will be down in a minute."

The children jumped up gladly, and slid down the roof. Clover fetched a couple of baskets from the woodshed. Elsie ran for her kitten. Dorry and John loaded themselves with two great faggots of green boughs. Just as they were ready the side door banged, and Katy and Cecy Hall came into the yard.

I must tell you about Cecy. She was a great friend of the children's, and lived in a house next door. The yards of the houses were only separated by a green hedge, with no gate, so that Cecy spent two-thirds of her time at Dr. Carr's, and was exactly like one of the family. She was a neat, dapper, pink-and-white girl, modest and prim in manner, with light shiny hair, which always kept smooth, and slim hands, which never looked dirty. How different from my poor Katy! Katy's hair was for ever untidy; her gowns were always catching on nails and "tearing themselves"; and, in spite of her age and size, she was as heedless and innocent as a child of six. Katy was the *longest* girl that was ever seen. What she did to make herself grow so, nobody could tell; but there she was—up above Papa's ear, and half a head taller than poor Aunt Izzie. Whenever she stopped to think about her height she became very awkward, and felt as if she were all legs and elbows, and angles and joints. Happily, her head was so full of other things, of plans and schemes and fancies of all sorts, that she didn't often take time to remember how tall she was. She was a dear, loving child, for all her careless habits, and made bushels of good resolutions every week of her life, only unluckily she never kept any of them. She had fits of responsibility about the other children, and longed to set them a good example, but when the chance came she generally forgot to do so. Katy's days flew like the wind; for when she wasn't studying lessons, or sewing and darning with Aunt Izzie, which she hated extremely, there were always so many delightful schemes rioting in her brains, that all she wished for was ten pairs of hands to carry them out. These same active brains got her into perpetual scrapes. She was fond of building castles in the air, and dreaming of the time when something she had done would make her famous, so that everybody would hear of her, and want to know her. I don't think she had made up her mind what this wonderful thing was to be; but while thinking about it she often forgot to learn a lesson, or to lace her boots, and then she had a bad mark, or a scolding from Aunt Izzie. At such times she consoled herself with planning how, by and by, she would be beautiful and beloved, and amiable as an angel. A great deal was to happen to Katy before that time came. Her eyes, which were black, were to turn blue; her nose was to lengthen and straighten, and her mouth, quite too large at present to suit the part of a heroine, was to be made over into a sort of rosy button. Meantime, and until these charming changes should take place, Katy forgot her features as much as she could, though still, I think, the person on earth whom she most envied was that lady on the outside of the Tricopherous bottles with the wonderful hair which sweeps the ground.

CHAPTER TWO

PARADISE

The place to which the children were going was a sort of marshy thicket at the bottom of a field near the house. It wasn't a big thicket, but it looked big, because the trees and bushes grew so closely that you could not see just where it ended. In winter the ground was damp and boggy, so that nobody went there, excepting cows, who don't mind getting their feet wet; but in summer the water dried away, and then it was all fresh and green, and full of delightful things—wild roses and sassafras and birds' nests. Narrow, winding paths ran here and there, made by the cattle as they wandered to and fro. This place the children called "Paradise", and to them it seemed as wild and endless and full of adventure as any forest of fairy-land.

The way to Paradise was through some wooden bars. Katy and Cecy climbed these with a hop, skip, and jump, while the smaller ones scrambled underneath. Once past the bars they were fairly in the field, and, with one consent, they all began to run till they reached the entrance of the wood. Then they halted with a queer look of hesitation on their faces. It was always an exciting occasion to go to Paradise for the first time after the long winter. Who knew what the fairies might not have done since any of them had been there to see?

"Which path shall we go in by?" asked Clover at last.

"Suppose we vote," said Katy. "I say by the Pilgrim's Path and the Hill of Difficulty."

"So do I!" chimed in Clover, who always agreed with Katy.

"The Path of Peace is nice," suggested Cecy.

"No, no! We want to go by Sassafras Path!" cried John and Dorry.

However, Katy as usual had her way. It was agreed that they should first try Pilgrim's Path, and afterward make a thorough exploration of the whole of their little kingdom, and see all that had happened since last they were there. So in they marched, Katy and Cecy heading the procession, and Dorry, with his great trailing bunch of boughs, bringing up the rear.

"Oh, there is the dear Rosary, all safe!" cried the children as they reached the top of the Hill of Difficulty, and came upon a tall stump, out of the middle of which waved a wild rose bush, budded over with fresh green leaves. This "Rosary" was a fascinating thing to their minds. They were always inventing stories about it, and were in constant terror lest some hungry cow should take a fancy to the rose bush and eat it up.

"Yes," said Katy, stroking a leaf with her finger, "it was in great danger one night last winter, but it escaped."

"Oh! how? Tell us about it!" cried the others, for Katy's stories were famous in the family.

14

"It was Christmas Eve," continued Katy in a mysterious tone. "The fairy of the Rosary was quite sick. She had taken a dreadful cold in her head, and the poplar-tree fairy, just over there, told her that sassafras tea is good for colds. So she made a large acorn-cup full, and then cuddled herself in where the wood looks so black and soft, and fell asleep. In the middle of the night, when she was snoring soundly, there was a noise in the forest, and a dreadful black bull with fiery eyes galloped up. He saw our poor Rosy Posy, and, opening his big mouth, he was just going to bite her in two; but at that minute a little fat man, with a wand in his hand, popped out from behind the stump. It was Santa Claus, of course. He gave the bull such a rap with his wand that he moo-ed dreadfully, and then put up his fore-paw to see if his nose was on or not. He found it was, but it hurt him so that he moo-ed again, and galloped off as fast as he could farther into the woods. Then Santa Claus woke up the fairy, and told her that if she didn't take better care of Rosy Posy he should put some other fairy into her place, and set her to keep guard over a prickly, scratchy, blackberry bush."

"Is there really any fairy?" asked Dorry, who had listened to this narrative with open mouth.

"Of course," answered Katy. Then bending down toward Dorry, she added in a voice intended to be of wonderful sweetness: "I am a fairy, Dorry!"

"Pshaw!" was Dorry's reply; "you're a giraffe—Papa said so!"

The Path of Peace got its name because of its darkness and coolness. High bushes almost met over it, and trees kept it shady, even in the middle of the day. A sort of white flower grew there, which the children called Pollypods, because they didn't know the real name. They stayed a long while picking bunches of these flowers, and then John and Dorry had to grub up an armful of sassafras roots; so that before they had fairly gone through Toadstool Avenue, Rabbit Hollow, and the rest, the sun was just over their heads, and it was noon.

"I'm getting hungry," said Dorry.

"Oh no, Dorry, you mustn't be hungry till the bower is ready!" cried the little girls, alarmed, for Dorry was apt to be disconsolate if he was kept waiting for his meals. So they made haste to build the bower. It did not take long, being composed of boughs hung over skipping-ropes, which were tied to the very poplar tree where the fairy lived who had recommended sassafras tea to the Fairy of the Rose.

When it was one they all cuddled in underneath. It was a very small bower—just big enough to hold them, and the baskets, and the kitten. I don't think there would have been room for anybody else, not even another kitten. Katy, who sat in the middle, untied and lifted the lid of the largest basket, while all the rest peeped eagerly to see what was inside.

First came a great many ginger cakes. These were carefully laid on the grass to keep till wanted. Buttered biscuits came next—three apiece, with slices of cold lamb laid in between; and last of all were a dozen hard-boiled eggs, and a layer of thick bread and butter sandwiched with corned beef. Aunt Izzie had put up lunches for Paradise before, you see, and knew pretty well what to expect in the way of appetite.

Oh, how good everything tasted in that bower, with the fresh wind rustling the poplar leaves, sunshine and sweet wood smells about them, and birds singing overhead! No grown-up dinner party ever had half so much fun. Each mouthful was a pleasure; and when the last crumb had vanished Katy produced the second

16

basket, and there, oh, delightful surprise! were seven little pies—molasses pies, baked in saucers—each with a brown top and crisp candified edge, which tasted like toffee and lemon-peel, and all sorts of good things mixed up together.

There was a general shout. Even demure Cecy was pleased, and Dorry and John kicked their heels on the ground in a tumult of joy. Seven pairs of hands were held out at once towards the basket; seven sets of teeth went to work without a moment's delay. In an incredibly short time every vestige of pie had disappeared, and a blissful stickiness pervaded the party.

"What shall we do now" asked Clover, while little Phil tipped the baskets upside-down, as if to make sure there was nothing left that could possibly be eaten.

"I don't know," replied Katy dreamily. She had left her seat, and was half sitting, half lying on the low, crooked bough of a butternut tree, which hung almost over the children's heads.

"Let's play we're grown up," said Cecy, "and tell what we mean to do."

"Well," said Clover, "you begin. What do you mean to do?"

"I mean to have a black silk dress, and pink roses in my bonnet, and a white muslin long-shawl," said Cecy; "and I mean to look *exactly* like Minerva Clark! I shall be very good too; as good as Mrs. Bedell, only a great deal prettier. All the young gentlemen will want me to go and ride, but I shan't notice them at all, because you know I shall always be teaching in Sunday-school and visiting the poor. And some day, when I am bending over an old woman and feeding her with currant jelly, a poet will come along and see me, and he'll go home and write a poem about me," concluded Cecy triumphantly.

"Pooh!" said Clover. "I don't think that would be nice at all. *I'm* going to be a beautiful lady—the most beautiful lady in the world! And I'm going to live in a yellow castle, with yellow pillars to the portico, and a square thing on top, like Mr. Sawyer's. My children are going to have a playhouse up there. There's going to be a spy-glass in the window, to look out of. I shall wear gold dresses and silver dresses every day, and diamond rings, and have white satin aprons to tie on when I'm dusting or do anything dirty. In the middle of my back-yard there will be a pond full of eau de Cologne, and whenever I want any I shall just go out and dip a bottle in. And I shan't teach in Sunday-schools like Cecy, because I don't want to; but every Sunday I'll go and stand by the gate, and when her scholars go by on their way home, I'll put eau de Cologne on their handkerchiefs."

"I mean to have just the same," cried Elsie, whose imagination was fired by this gorgeous vision, "only my pond will be the biggest. I shall be a great deal beautifuller, too," she added.

"You can't," said Katy from overhead. "Clover is going to be the most beautiful lady in the world."

"But I'll be *more* beautiful than the most beautiful," persisted poor little Elsie; "and I'll be big too, and know everybody's secrets. And everybody'll be kind then, and never run away and hide; and there won't be any post offices or anything disagreeable."

"What'll you be, Johnnie?" asked Clover, anxious to change the subject, for Elsie's voice was growing plaintive.

But Johnnie had no clear ideas as to her future. She laughed a great deal, and squeezed Dorry's arm very tight, but that was all. Dorry was more explicit.

"I mean to have turkey every day," he declared, "and batter puddings; not boiled ones, you know, but little baked ones, with brown shiny tops, and a great deal of pudding sauce to eat on them. And I shall be so big then that nobody will say, 'Three helps is quite enough for a little boy'."

"Oh, Dorry, you pig!" cried Katy, while the others screamed with laughter. Dorry was much affronted.

"I shall just go and tell Aunt Izzie what you called me," he said, getting up in a great pet.

But Clover, who was a born peacemaker, caught hold of his arm, and her coaxings and entreaties consoled him so much that he finally said he would stay; especially as the others were quite grave now, and promised that they wouldn't laugh any more.

"And now, Katy, it's your turn," said Cecy; "tell us what you're going to be when you grow up."

"I'm not sure about what I'll be," replied Katy from overhead; "beautiful, of course, and good if I can, only not so good as you, Cecy, because it would be nice to go and ride with the young gentlemen *sometimes*. And I'd like to have a large house and a splendiferous garden, and then you could all come and live with me, and we would play in the garden, and Dorry should have turkey five times a day if he liked. And we'd have a machine to darn the stockings, and another machine to put the bureau drawers in order, and we'd never sew or knit garters, or do anything we didn't want to. That's what I'd like to *be*. But now I'll tell you what I mean to *do*."

"Isn't it the same thing?" asked Cecy.

"Oh no!" replied Katy, "quite different; for you see I mean to *do* something grand. I don't know what, yet; but when I'm grown up I shall find out." (Poor Katy always said "when I'm grown up," forgetting how very much she had grown already.) "Perhaps," she went on, "it will be rowing out in boats, and saving people's lives, like that girl in the book. Or perhaps I shall go and nurse in the hospital, like Miss Nightingale. Or else I'll head a crusade and ride on a white horse, with armour and a helmet on my head, and carry a sacred flag. Or if I don't do that, I'll paint pictures or sing or scalp—sculp—what is it? you know— make figures in marble. Anyhow, it shall be *something*. And when Aunt Izzie sees it, and reads about me in the newspapers, she will say, 'The dear child I always knew she would turn out an ornament to the family.' People very often say, afterwards, that they 'always knew'," concluded Katy sagaciously.

"Oh, Katy, how beautiful it will be!" said Clover, clasping her hands. Clover believed in Katy as she did in the Bible.

"I don't believe the newspapers will be so silly as to print things about *you*, Katy Carr," put in Elsie vindictively.

"Yes they will!" said Clover; and gave Elsie a push.

By and by John and Dorry trotted away on mysterious errands of their own.

"Wasn't Dorry funny with his turkey?" remarked Cecy; and they all laughed again.

"If you won't tell," said Katy, "I'll let you see Dorry's journal. He kept it once for almost two weeks, and then gave it up. I found the book, this morning, in the nursery closet."

All of them promised, and Katy produced it from her pocket. It began thus:

"March 12.—Have resolved to keep a journal.

"March 13.—Had rost befe for diner, and cabage, and potato and appel sawse, and rice puding. I do not like rice puding when it is like ours. Charley Slack's kind is rele good. Mush and sirup for tea.

"March 19.—Forgit what did John and me saved our pie to take to schule.

"March 21.—Forgit what did. Gridel cakes for brekfast. Debby didn't fry enuff.

"*March 24.*—This is Sunday. Corn befe for dinnir. Studdied my Bibel leson. Aunt Issy said I was gredy. Have resollved not to think so much about things to ete. Wish I was a beter boy. Nothing pertikeler for tea.

"*March 25.*—Forgit what did.

"*March 27.*—Forgit what did.

"*March 29.*—Played.

"*March 31.*—Forgit what did.

"*April 1.*—Have dissided not to kepe a jurnal enny more."

Here ended the extracts; and it seemed as if only a minute had passed since they stopped laughing over them, before the long shadows began to fall, and Mary came to say that all of them must come in to get ready for tea. It was dreadful to have to pick up the empty baskets and go home, feeling that the long, delightful Saturday was over, and that there wouldn't be another for a week. But it was comforting to remember that Paradise was always there; and that at any moment, when Fate and Aunt Izzie were willing, they had only to climb a pair of bars—very easy ones, and without any fear of an angel with flaming sword to stop the way—enter in, and take possession of their Eden.

CHAPTER THREE

THE DAY OF SCRAPES

Mrs. Knight's school, to which Katy and Clover and Cecy went, stood quite at the other end of the town from Dr. Carr's. It was a low, one-storey building, and had a yard behind it, in which the girls played at recess. Unfortunately, next door to it was Miss Miller's school, equally large and popular, and with a yard behind it also. Only a high board fence separated the two playgrounds.

Mrs. Knight was a stout, gentle woman, who moved slowly, and had a face which made you think of an amiable and well-disposed cow. Miss Miller, on the contrary, had black eyes, with black corkscrew curls waving about them, and was generally brisk and snappy. A constant feud raged between the two schools as to the respective merits of the teachers and the instruction. The Knight girls, for some unknown reason, considered themselves genteel and the Miller girls vulgar, and took no pains to conceal this opinion; while the Miller girls, on the other hand, retaliated by being as aggravating as they knew how. They spent their recesses and intermissions mostly in making faces through the knot-holes in the fence, and over the top of it when they could get there, which wasn't an easy thing to do, as the fence was pretty high. The Knight girls could make faces too, for all their gentility. Their yard had one great advantage over the other: it possessed a woodshed, with a climbable roof, which commanded Miss Miller's premises, and upon this the girls used to sit in rows, turning up their noses at the next yard, and irritating the foe by jeering remarks. "Knights" and "Millerites", the two schools called each other; and the feud raged so high, that sometimes it was hardly safe for a Knight to meet a Millerite in the street; all of which, as may be imagined, was exceedingly improving both to the manners and morals of the young ladies concerned!

One morning, not long after the day in Paradise,

Katy was late. She could not find her things. Her algebra, as she expressed it, had "gone and lost itself", her slate was missing, and the string was off her sun-bonnet. She ran about, searching for these articles and banging doors, till Aunt Izzie was out of patience.

"As for your algebra," she said, "if it is that very dirty book with only one cover, and scribbled all over the leaves, you will find it under the kitchen table. Philly was playing before breakfast that it was a pig: no wonder, I'm sure, for it looks good for nothing else. How you do manage to spoil your school books in this manner, Katy, I cannot imagine. It is less than a month since your father got you a new algebra, and look at it now—not fit to be carried about. I do wish you would realize what books cost!"

"About your slate," she went on, "I know nothing; but here is the bonnet-string," taking it out of her pocket.

"Oh, thank you!" said Katy, hastily sticking it on with a pin.

"Katy Carr!" almost screamed Miss Izzie. "What *are* you about? Pinning on your bonnet-string! Mercy on me, what shiftless thing will you do next? Now stand still, and don't fidget! You shan't stir till I have sewed it on properly."

It wasn't easy to "stand still and not fidget", with Aunt Izzie fussing away and lecturing, and now and then, in a moment of forgetfulness, sticking her needle into one's chin. Katy bore it as well as she could, only shifting perpetually from one foot to the other, and now and then uttering a little snort, like an impatient horse. The minute she was released she flew into the kitchen, seized the algebra, and rushed like a whirl-wind to the gate, where good little Clover stood patiently waiting, though all ready herself, and terribly afraid she should be late.

"We shall have to run!" gasped Katy, quite out of breath. "Aunt Izzie kept me! She has been so horrid!"

They did run as fast as they could, but time ran faster, and before they were half way to school the town clock struck nine, and all hope was over. This vexed Katy very much; for, though often late, she was always eager to be early.

"There," she said, stopping short. "I shall just tell Aunt Izzie that it was her fault. It is *too* bad." And she marched into school in a very cross mood.

A day begun in this manner is pretty sure to end badly, as most of us know. All the morning through things seemed to go wrong. Katy missed twice in her grammar lesson, and lost her place in the class. Her hand shook so when she copied her composition, that the writing, not good at best, turned out almost illegible, so that Mrs. Knight said it must all be done over again. This made Katy crosser than ever-and almost before she thought, she had whispered to Clover, "How hateful!" And then, when just before recess all who had "whispered" were requested to stand up, her conscience gave such a twinge that she was forced to get up with the rest, and see a black mark put against her name on the list. The tears came into her eyes from vexation; and, for fear the other girls would notice them, she made a bolt for the yard as soon as the bell rang, and mounted up all alone to the wood-house roof, where she sat with her back to the school, fighting with her eyes, and trying to get her face in order before the rest should come.

Miss Miller's clock was about four minutes slower than Mrs. Knight's, so the next playground was empty. It was a warm, breezy day, and as Katy sat there, suddenly a gust of wind came, and seizing her sunbonnet, which was only half tied on, whirled it across the roof. She clutched after it as it flew, but too late.

24

Once, twice, thrice it flapped, then it disappeared over the edge, and Katy, flying after, saw it lying a crumpled lilac heap in the very middle of the enemy's yard.

This was horrible. Not merely losing the bonnet, for Katy was comfortably indifferent as to what became of her clothes, but to lose it *so*. In another minute the Miller girls would be out. Already she seemed to see them dancing war-dances round the unfortunate bonnet, pinning it on a pole, using it as a football, waving it over the fence, and otherwise treating it as Indians treat a captive taken in war. Was it to be endured? Never! Better die first! And with very much the feeling of a person who faces destruction rather than forfeit honour, Katy set her teeth, and sliding rapidly down the roof, seized the fence, and with one bold leap vaulted into Miss Miller's yard.

Just then the recess bell tinkled; and a little Millerite who sat by the window, and who, for two seconds, had been dying to give the exciting information, squeaked out to the others: "There's Katy Carr in our back-yard!"

Out poured the Millerites, big and little. Their wrath and indignation at this daring invasion cannot be described. With a howl of fury they precipitated themselves upon Katy, but she was quick as they, and, holding the rescued bonnet in her hand, was already half way up the fence.

There are moments when it is a fine thing to be tall. On this occasion Katy's long legs and arms served her an excellent turn. Nothing but a Daddy-long-legs ever climbed so fast or so wildly as she did now. In one second she had gained the top of the fence. Just as she went over a Millerite seized her by the last foot, and almost dragged her boot off.

Almost, not quite, thanks to the stout thread with which Aunt Izzie had sewed the buttons on. With a frantic kick Katy released herself, and had the satisfaction of seeing her assailant go head over heels backwards, while, with a shriek of triumph and fright, she herself plunged headlong into the midst of a group of Knights. They were listening with open mouths to the uproar, and now stood transfixed at the astonishing spectacle of one of their number absolutely returning alive from the camp of the enemy.

I cannot tell you what a commotion ensued. The Knights were beside themselves with pride and triumph. Katy was kissed and hugged, and made to tell her story over and over again, while rows of exulting girls sat on the wood-house roof to crow over the discomfited Millerites: and when, later, the foe rallied and began to retort over the fence, Clover, armed with a tack-hammer, was lifted up in the arms of one of the tall girls to rap the intruding knuckles as they appeared on the top. This she did with such goodwill that the Millerites were glad to drop down again, and mutter vengeance at a safe distance. Altogether it was a great day for the school, a day to be remembered. As time went on, Katy, what with the excitement of her adventure, and of being praised and petted by the big girls, grew perfectly reckless, and hardly knew what she said or did.

A good many of the scholars lived too far from school to go home at noon, and were in the habit of bringing their lunches in baskets, and staying all day. Katy and Clover were of this number. This noon, after the dinners were eaten, it was proposed that they should play something in the school-room, and Katy's unlucky star put it into her head to invent a new game, which she called the Game of Rivers.

It was played in the following manner: Each girl took the name of a river, and laid out for herself an appointed path through the room, winding among the desks and benches, and making a low, roaring sound, to imitate the noise of water. Cecy was the Platte; Marianne Brookes, a tall girl, the Mississippi; Alice Blair, the Ohio; Clover, the Penobscot; and so on. They were instructed to run into each other once in a while, because, as Katy said, "rivers do".

As for Katy herself, she was "Father Ocean" and, growling horribly, raged up and down the platform where Mrs. Knight usually sat. Every now and then, when the others were at the far end of the room, she would suddenly cry out, "Now for a meeting of the waters!" whereupon all the rivers, bouncing, bounding, scrambling, screaming, would turn and run toward the Ocean, while he roared louder than all of them put together, and made short rushes up and down, to represent the movement of waves on a beach.

Such a noise as this beautiful game made was never heard in the town of Burnet before or since. It was like the bellowing of the bulls of Bashan, the squeaking of pigs, the cackle of turkey-cocks, and the laugh of wild hyenas all at once; and, in addition, there was a great banging of furniture and scraping of many feet on an uncarpeted floor. People going by stopped and stared, children cried, and an old lady asked why someone didn't run for a policeman; while the Miller girls listened with malicious pleasure, and told everybody that it was the noise that Mrs. Knight's scholars "usually made at recess".

Mrs. Knight coming back from dinner was much amazed to see a crowd of people collected in front of her school. As she drew near, the sounds reached her, and then she became really frightened, for she thought somebody was being murdered on her premises. Hurrying in, she threw open the door, and there, to her

27

dismay, was the whole room in a frightful state of confusion and uproar: chairs flung down, desks upset, ink streaming on the floor; while in the midst of the ruin the frantic rivers raced and screamed, and Old Father Ocean, with a face as red as fire, capered like a lunatic on the platform.

"What *does* this mean?" gasped poor Mrs. Knight, almost unable to speak for horror.

At the sound of her voice the Rivers stood still! Father Ocean brought his prances to an abrupt close, and slunk down from the platform. All of a sudden each girl seemed to realize what a condition the room was in, and what a horrible thing she had done. The timid ones cowered behind their desks, the bold ones tried to look unconscious and, to make matters worse, the scholars who had gone home to dinner began to return, staring at the scene of disaster, and asking, in whispers, what had been going on?

Mrs. Knight rang the bell. When the school had come to order, she had the desks and chairs picked up, while she herself brought wet cloths to sop the ink from the floor. This was done in profound silence; and the expression on Mrs. Knight's face was so direful and solemn, that a fresh damp fell upon the spirits of the guilty Rivers, and Father Ocean wished himself thousands of miles away.

When all was in order again, and the girls had taken their seats, Mrs. Knight made a short speech. She said she never was so shocked in her life before; she had supposed that she could trust them to behave like ladies when her back was turned. The idea that they could act so disgracefully, make such an uproar, and alarm people going by, had never occurred to her, and she was deeply pained. It was setting a bad example to all the neighbourhood—by-which Mrs. Knight meant the rival school, Miss Miller having just sent over a little girl, with her compliments, to ask if anyone was hurt, and could *she* do anything? which was naturally aggravating! Mrs. Knight hoped they were sorry; she thought they must be—sorry and ashamed. The exercises could now go on as usual. Of course some punishment would be incited for the offence, but she should have to reflect before deciding what it ought to be. Meantime she wanted them all to think it over seriously; and if anyone felt that she was more to blame than the others, now was the moment to rise and confess it.

Katy's heart gave a great thump, but she rose bravely: "I made up the game, and I was Father Ocean," she said to the astonished Mrs. Knight, who glared at her for a minute, and then replied solemnly, "Very well, Katy—sit down"; which Katy did, feeling more ashamed than ever, but somehow relieved in her mind. There is a saving grace in truth which helps truth-tellers through the worst of their troubles, and Katy found this out now.

The afternoon was long and hard. Mrs. Knight did not smile once; the lessons dragged; and Katy, after the heat and excitement of the forenoon, began to feel miserable. She had received more than one hard blow during the meetings of the waters, and had bruised herself almost without knowing it, against the desks and chairs. All these places now began to ache: her head throbbed so that she could hardly see, and a lump of something heavy seemed to be lying on her heart.

When school was over Mrs. Knight rose and said: "The young ladies who took part in the game this afternoon are requested to remain." All the others went away, and shut the door behind them. It was a horrible moment: the girls never forgot it, or the hopeless sound of the door as the last departing scholar clapped it after her as she left.

I can't begin to tell you what it was that Mrs. Knight said to them; it was very affecting, and before long most of the girls began to cry. The penalty for their offence was announced to be the loss of recess for three weeks; but that wasn't half so bad as seeing Mrs. Knight so "religious and afflicted", as Cecy told her mother afterwards. One by one the sobbing sinners departed from the school-room. When most of them were gone Mrs. Knight called Katy up to the platform, and said a few words to her specially. She was not really severe, but Katy was too penitent and worn out to bear much, and before long was weeping like a waterspout, or like the ocean she had pretended to be.

At this, tender-hearted Mrs. Knight was so much affected that she let her off at once, and even kissed her in token of forgiveness, which made poor Ocean sob harder than ever. All the way home she sobbed; faithful little Clover, running along by her side in great distress, begging her to stop crying, and trying in vain to hold up the fragments of her dress, which was torn in at least a dozen places. Katy could not stop crying, and it was fortunate that Aunt Izzie happened to be out, and that the only person who saw her in this piteous plight was Mary, the nurse, who doted on the children, and was always ready to help them out of their troubles.

On this occasion she petted and cossetted Katy exactly as if it had been Johnnie or little Phil. She took her on her lap, bathed the hot head, brushed the hair, put arnica on the bruises, and produced a clean frock, so that by tea time the poor child, except for her red eyes, looked like herself again, and Aunt Izzie didn't notice anything unusual.

For a wonder, Dr. Carr was at home that evening. It was always a great treat to the children when this happened, and Katy thought herself happy when, after the little ones had gone to bed, she got Papa to herself, and told him the whole story.

"Papa," she said, sitting on his knee, which, big girl as she was, she liked very much to do, "what is the reason that makes some days so lucky and other days so unlucky? Now, today began all wrong, and everything that happened in it was wrong; and on other days I begin right, and all goes right, straight through. If Aunt Izzie hadn't kept me in the morning, I shouldn't have lost my mark, and then I shouldn't have been cross, and then *perhaps* I shouldn't have got into my other scrapes."

"But what made Aunt Izzie keep you, Katy?"

"To sew on the string of my bonnet, Papa."

"But how did it happen that the string was off?"

"Well," said Katy reluctantly, "I am afraid that was *my* fault, for it came off on Tuesday, and I didn't fasten it on."

"So you see we must go back before Aunt Izzie for the beginning of this unlucky day of yours, Child. Did you ever hear the old saying 'For the want of a nail the shoe was lost'?"

"No, never—tell it to me!" cried Katy, who loved stories as well as when she was three years old.

So Dr. Carr repeated:

> "For the want of a nail the shoe was lost,
> For the want of a shoe the horse was lost,
> For the want of a horse the rider was lost,
> For the want of the rider the battle was lost,
> For the want of the battle the kingdom was lost,
> And all for want of a horse-shoe nail."

"Oh, Papa!" exclaimed Katy, giving him a great hug as she got off his knee, "I see what you mean! Who would have thought such a little speck of a thing as not sewing on my string could make a difference? But I don't believe I shall get into any more scrapes, for I shan't ever forget:

'For the want of a nail the shoe was lost'."

CHAPTER FOUR

KIKERI

But I am sorry to say that my poor, thoughtless Katy *did* forget, and did get into another scrape, and that no later than the very next Monday.

Monday was apt to be rather a stormy day at the Carrs'. There was the big wash to be done, and Aunt Izzie always seemed a little harder to please, and the servants a good deal crosser than on common days. But I think it was also, in part, the fault of the children, who, after the quiet of Sunday, were specially frisky and uproarious, and readier than usual for all sorts of mischief.

To Clover and Elsie, Sunday seemed to begin at Saturday's bed time, when their hair was wet, and screwed up in papers, that it might curl next day. Elsie's waved naturally, so Aunt Izzie didn't think it necessary to pin her papers very tight; but Clover's thick, straight locks required to be pinched hard before they would give even the least twirl, and to her Saturday night was one of misery. She would lie tossing and turning, and trying first one side of her head and then the other; but whichever way she placed herself, the hard knobs and the pins stuck out and hurt her; so when at last she fell asleep, it was face down, with her small nose buried in the pillow, which was not comfortable, and gave her bad dreams. In consequence of these sufferings Clover hated curls, and when she "made up" stories for the younger children, they always commenced: "The hair of the beautiful princess was as straight as a yard-stick, and she never did it up in papers—never!"

Sunday always began with a Bible story, followed by a breakfast of baked beans, which two things were much tangled up together in Philly's mind. After breakfast the children studied their Sunday-school lessons, and then the big wagonette came round, and they drove to church, which was a good mile o. It was a large, old-fashioned church, with galleries, and long pews with high red-cushioned seats. The choir sat at the end, behind a low, green curtain, which slipped from side to side on rods. When the sermon began, they would draw the curtain aside and show themselves, all ready to listen, but the rest of the time they kept it shut. Katy always guessed that they must be having good times behind the green curtain—eating orange-peel, perhaps, or reading the Sunday-school books—and she often wished she might sit up there among them.

The seat in Dr. Carr's pew was so high that none of the children, except Katy, could touch the floor, even with the point of a toe. This made their feet go to sleep; and when they felt the queer little pin-pricks which drowsy feet use to rouse themselves with, they would slide off the seat, and sit on the benches to get over it. Once there, and well hidden from view, it was almost impossible not to whisper. Aunt Izzie would frown and shake her head, but it did little good, especially as Phil and Dorry were sleeping with their heads on her lap, and it took both her hands to keep them from rolling off into the bottom of the pew. When good old Dr. Stone said, "Finally, my brethren," she would begin waking them up. It was hard work sometimes, but generally she succeeded, so that during the last hymn the two stood together on the seat, quite brisk and refreshed, sharing a hymn-book, and making believe to sing like the older people.

After church came Sunday-school, which the children liked very much, and then they went home to dinner, which was always the same on Sunday—cold corned beef, baked potatoes, and rice pudding. They did not go to church in the afternoon unless they wished, but were pounced upon by Katy instead, and forced to listen to the reading of *The Sunday Visitor*, a religious paper, of which she was the editor. This paper was partly written, partly printed, on a large sheet of foolscap and had at the top an ornamental device, in lead pencil, with "Sunday Visitor" in the middle of it. The reading part began with a dull little piece of the kind which grown people call an editorial, about "Neatness", or "Obedience", or "Punctuality". The children always fidgeted when listening to this, partly, I think, because it aggravated them to have Katy recommending on paper, as very easy, the virtues which she herself found it so hard to practise in real life. Next came anecdotes about dogs and elephants and snakes, taken from the Natural History book, and not very interesting, because the audience knew them by heart already. A hymn or two followed, or a string of original verses, and, last of all, a chapter of "Little Maria and Her Sisters", a dreadful tale, in which Katy drew so much moral, and made such personal allusions to the faults of the rest, that it was almost more than they could bear. In fact, there had just been a nursery rebellion on the subject. You must know that, for some weeks back, Katy had been too lazy to prepare any fresh *Sunday Visitors*, and so had forced the children to sit in a row and listen to the back numbers, which she read aloud from the very beginning! "Little Maria" sounded much worse when taken in these large doses, and Clover and Elsie, combining for once, made up their minds to endure it no longer. So, watching their chance, they carried o the whole edition, and poked it into the kitchen fire, where they watched it burn with a mixture of fear and delight which it was comical to witness. They dared not confess the deed, but it was impossible not to look conscious when Katy was flying about and rummaging after her lost treasure, and she suspected them, and was very irate in consequence.

The evenings of Sundays were always spent in repeating hymns to Papa and Aunt Izzie. This was fun, for they all took turns, and there was quite a scramble as to who should secure the favourites, such as "The west hath shut its gate of gold" and "Go when the morning shineth". On the whole, Sunday was a sweet and pleasant day, and the children thought so; but, from its being so much quieter than other days, they always got up on Monday full of life and mischief, and ready to fizz over at any minute, like champagne bottles with the wires just cut.

This particular Monday was rainy, so there couldn't be any outdoor play, which was the usual vent for over-high spirits. The little ones, cooped up in the nursery all the afternoon, had grown perfectly riotous. Philly was not quite well, and had been taking medicine. The medicine was called "Elixir Pro." It was a great favourite with Aunt Izzie, who kept a bottle of it always on hand. The bottle was large and black, with a paper label tied round its neck, and the children shuddered at the sight of it.

After Phil had stopped roaring and spluttering, and play had begun again, the dolls, as was only natural, were taken ill also, and so was "Pikery," John's little yellow chair, which she always pretended was a doll too. She kept an old apron tied on his back, and generally took him to bed with her—not *into* bed, that would have been troublesome, but close by, tied to the bed-post. Now, as she told the others, Pikery was very sick indeed. He must have some medicine, just like Philly.

"Give him some water," suggested Dorry.

"No," said John decidedly, "it must be black and out of a bottle, or it won't do any good."

After thinking a moment, she trotted quietly across the passage into Aunt Izzie's room. Nobody was there, but John knew where the Elixir Pro was kept—in the closet on the third shelf. She pulled one of the drawers out a little, climbed up, and fetched it down. The children were enchanted when she marched back, the bottle in one hand, the cork in the other, and proceeded to pour a liberal dose on to Pikery's wooden seat, which John called his lap.

"There! there! my poor boy," she said, patting his shoulder—I mean his arm "swallow it down—it'll do you good."

Just then Aunt Izzie came in, and to her dismay saw a long trickle of something dark and sticky running down on to the carpet. It was Pikery's medicine, which he had refused to swallow.

"What is that?" she asked sharply.

"My baby is sick," faltered John, displaying the guilty bottle.

Aunt Izzie rapped her over the head with a thimble, and told her that she was a very naughty child, whereupon Johnnie pouted and cried a little. Aunt Izzie wiped up the slop, and, taking away the Elixir, retired with it to her closet, saying that she "never knew anything like it—it was always so on Mondays."

What further pranks were played in the nursery that day I cannot pretend to tell. But late in the afternoon a dreadful screaming was heard, and when people rushed from all parts of the house to see what was the matter, behold the nursery door was locked, and nobody could get in. Aunt Izzie called through the keyhole to have it opened, but the roars were so loud that it was long before she could get an answer. At last Elsie, sobbing violently, explained that Dorry had locked the door, and now the key wouldn't turn, and they couldn't open it. *Would* they have to stay there always and starve?

"Of course you won't, you foolish child!" exclaimed Aunt Izzie. "Dear, dear, what on earth will come next? Stop crying, Elsie; do you hear me? You shall all be got out in a few minutes."

And sure enough, the next thing came a rattling at the blinds, and there was Alexander, the hired man, standing outside on a tall ladder and nodding his head at the children. The little ones forgot their fright. They flew to open the window, and frisked and jumped about Alexander as he climbed in and unlocked the door. It struck them as being such a fine thing to be let out in this way, that Dorry began to rather plume himself for fastening them in.

But Aunt Izzie didn't take this view of the case. She scolded them well, and declared they were troublesome children, who couldn't be trusted one moment out of sight, and that she was more than half sorry she had promised to go to the lecture that evening. "How do I know," she concluded, "that before I come home you won't have set the house on fire, or killed somebody?"

"O, no we won't! No we won't!" whined the children, quite moved by this frightful picture. But bless you—ten minutes afterwards they had forgotten all about it.

All this time Katy had been sitting on the ledge of the bookcase in the library, poring over a book. It was called Tasso's *Jerusalem Delivered*. The man who wrote it was an Italian, but somebody had done the story over into English. It was rather a queer book for a little girl to take a fancy to, but somehow Katy liked it very much. It told about knights. and ladies, and giants, and battles, and made her feel hot and cold by turns as she read, and as if she must rush at something, and shout, and strike blows.

Katy was naturally fond of reading. Papa encouraged it. He kept a few books locked up, and then turned her loose in the library. She read all sorts of things: travels and sermons, and old magazines. Nothing was so dull that she couldn't get through it. Anything really interesting absorbed her so that she never knew what was going on about her. The little girls to whose houses she went visiting had found this out, and always hid away their story-books when she was expected to tea. If they didn't do this, she was sure to pick one up and plunge in, and then it was no use

38

to call her or tug at her dress, for she neither saw nor heard anything more till it was time to go home.

This afternoon she read the *Jerusalem* till it was too dark to see any more. On her way upstairs she met Aunt Izzie, with bonnet and shawl on.

"Where *have* you been?" she said. "I have been calling you for the last half hour."

"I didn't hear you, ma'am."

"But where were you?" persisted Miss Izzie.

"In the library, reading," replied Katy.

Her aunt gave a sort of sniff, but she knew Katy's ways and said no more. " I'm going out to drink tea with Mrs. Hall and attend the evening lecture," she went on. "Be sure that Clover gets her lesson, and if Cecy comes over as usual you must send her home early. All of you must be in bed by nine."

"Yes'm," said Katy; but I fear she was not attending much, but thinking, in her secret soul, how jolly it was to have Aunt Izzie go out for once. Miss Carr was very faithful to her duties, she seldom left the children, even for an evening; so whenever she did they felt a certain sense of novelty and freedom, which was dangerous as well as pleasant.

Still, I am sure that on this occasion Katy meant no mischief. Like all excitable people, she seldom did *mean* to do wrong, she just did it when it came into her head. Supper passed off successfully, and all might have gone well had it not been that after the lessons were learned and Cecy had come in, they fell to talking about "Kikeri".

Kikeri was a game which had been very popular with them a year before. They had invented it themselves, and chosen for it this queer name out of an old fairy story. It was a sort of mixture of blind-man's-buff and tag—only instead of anyone's eyes being bandaged, they all played in the dark. One of the children would stay out in the hall, which was dimly lighted from the stairs, while the others hid themselves in the nursery. When they were all hidden, they would call out "Kikeri", as a signal for the one in the hall to come in and find them. Of course, coming from the light he could see nothing, while the others could see only dimly. It was very exciting to stand crouching up in a corner and watch the dark figure stumbling about and feeling to right and left, while every now and then somebody, just escaping his clutches, would slip past and gain the hall, which was "Freedom Castle," with a joyful shout of "Kikeri, Kikeri, Kikeri, Ki!" Whoever was caught had to take the place of the catcher or a long time this game was the delight of the Carr children; but so many scratches and black-and-blue spots came of it, and so many of the nursery things were thrown down and broken, that at last Aunt Izzie issued an order that it should not be played any more. This was almost a year since; but talking of it now put it into their heads to want to try it again.

"After all we didn't promise," said Cecy.

"No, and *Papa* never said a word about our not playing it," added Katy, to whom "Papa" was authority, and must always be minded, while Aunt Izzie might now and then be defied.

So they all went upstairs. Dorry and John, though half undressed, were allowed to join the game. Philly was fast asleep in another room.

It was certainly splendid fun. Once Clover climbed up on the mantelpiece and sat there, and when Katy, who was finder, groped about a little more wildly than usual, she caught hold of Clover's foot, and couldn't imagine where it came from. Dorry got a hard knock, and cried, and at another time Katy's dress caught on the bureau handle and was frightfully torn, but these were too much affairs of every day to interfere in the least with the pleasures of Kikeri. The fun and frolic seemed to grow greater the longer they played. In the excitement time went on much faster than any of them dreamed. Suddenly, in the midst of the noise, came a sound—the sharp distinct slam of the carriage door at the side entrance. Aunt Izzie had returned from her lecture!

The dismay and confusion of that moment! Cecy slipped downstairs like an eel, and fled on the wings of fear along the path which led to her home. Mrs. Hall, as she bade Aunt Izzie good night, and shut Dr. Carr's front door behind her with a bang, might have been struck with the singular fact that a distant bang came from her own front door like a sort of echo. But she was not a suspicious woman; and when she went upstairs there were Cecy's clothes neatly folded on a chair, and Cecy herself in bed, fast asleep, only with a little more colour than usual in her cheeks.

Meantime, Aunt Izzie was on *her* way upstairs, and such a panic prevailed in the nursery! Katy felt it, and basely scuttled off to her own room, where she went to bed with all possible speed. But the others found it much harder to go to bed; there were so many of them, all getting into each other's way, and with no lamp to see by. Dorry and John popped under the clothes half undressed, Elsie disappeared, and Clover, too late for either, and hearing Aunt Izzie's step in the hall, did this horrible thing—fell on her knees, with her face buried in a chair, and began to say her prayers very hard indeed.

Aunt Izzie, coming in with a candle in her hand, stood in the doorway, astonished at the spectacle. She sat down and waited for Clover to get through, while

Clover, on her part, didn't dare to get through, but went on repeating "Now I lay me" over and over again, in a sort of despair. At last Aunt Izzie said very grimly "That will do, Clover, you can get up!" and Clover rose, feeling like a culprit, which she was, for it was much naughtier to pretend to be praying than to disobey Aunt Izzie and be out of bed after ten o'clock, though I think Clover hardly understood this then.

Aunt Izzie at once began to undress her, and while doing so asked so many questions, that before long she had got at the truth of the whole matter. She gave Clover a sharp scolding, and leaving her to wash her tearful face, she went to the bed where John and Dorry lay, fast asleep, and snoring as conspicuously as they knew how. Something strange in the appearance of the bed made her look more closely; she lifted the clothes, and there, sure enough, they were half dressed, and with their school boots on!

Such a shake as Aunt Izzie gave the little scamps at this discovery would have roused a couple of dormice. Much against their will, John and Dorry were forced to wake up, and be slapped and scolded, and made ready for bed, Aunt Izzie standing over them all the while, like a dragon. She had just tucked them warmly in, when for the first time she missed Elsie.

"Where is my poor little Elsie?" she exclaimed.

"In bed," said Clover meekly.

"In bed!" repeated Aunt Izzie, much amazed. Then, stooping down, she gave a vigorous pull. The trundle-bed came into view and, sure enough, there was Elsie, in full dress, shoes and all, but so fast asleep that not all Aunt Izzie's shakes, and pinches, and calls, were able to rouse her. Her clothes were taken off, her boots unlaced, her night-gown put on; but through it all Elsie slept, and she was the only one of the children who did not get the scolding she deserved that dreadful night.

Katy did not even pretend to be asleep when Aunt Izzie went to her room. Her tardy conscience had awoken, and she was lying in bed, very miserable at having drawn the others into a scrape as well as herself, and at the failure of her last set of resolutions about "setting an example to the younger ones". So unhappy was she, that Aunt Izzie's severe words were almost a relief: and though she cried herself to sleep, it was rather from the burden of her own thoughts than because she had been scolded.

She cried even harder the next day, for Dr. Carr talked to her more seriously than he had ever done before. He reminded her of the time when her mamma died, and of how she said: "Katy must be a mamma to the little ones when she grows up". And he asked her if she didn't think the time had come for beginning to take this dear place towards the children. Poor Katy! She sobbed as if her heart would break at this, and though she made no promises, I think she was never quite so thoughtless again after that day. As for the rest, Papa called them together and made them distinctly understand that Kikeri was never to be played any more. It was so seldom that Papa forbade any games, however boisterous, that this order really made an impression on the unruly brood, and they have never played Kikeri again from that day to this.

CHAPTER FIVE

IN THE LOFT

"I declare," said Miss Petingill, laying down her work, "if them children don't beat all! What on earth *are* they going to do now?"

Miss Petingill was sitting in the little room in the back building, which she always had when she came to the Carrs for a week's mending and making over. She was the dearest, funniest old woman who ever went out sewing by the day. Her face was round, and somehow made you think of a very nice baked apple, it was so criss-crossed, and lined by a thousand good-natured puckers. She was small and wiry, and wore caps and a false front, which was just the colour of a dusty Newfoundland dog's back. Her eyes were dim, and she used spectacles; but for all that, she was an excellent worker. Everyone liked Miss Petingill, though Aunt Izzie *did* once say that her tongue "was hung in the middle". Aunt Izzie made this remark when she was in a temper, and was by no means prepared to have Phil walk up at once and request Miss Petingill to "stick it out", which she obligingly did, while the rest of the children crowded to look. They couldn't see that it was different from other tongues, but Philly persisted in finding something curious about it; there must be, you know—since it was hung in that queer way!

Wherever Miss Petingill went, all sorts of treasures went with her. The children liked to have her come, for it was as good as a fairy story, or the circus, to see her

44

things unpacked. Miss Petingill was very much afraid of burglars; she lay awake half the night listening for them, and nothing on earth would have persuaded her to go anywhere, leaving behind what she called her "plate". This stately word meant six old teaspoons, very thin and bright and sharp, and a butter-knife, whose handle set forth that it was "A testimonial of gratitude, for saving the life of Ethuriel Jobson, aged seven, on the occasion of his being attacked with quinsy sore throat". Miss Petingill was very proud of her knife. It and the spoons travelled about in a little basket which hung on her arm, and was never allowed to be out of her sight, even when the family she was sewing for were the honestest people in the world.

Then, beside the plate-basket, Miss Petingill never stirred without Tom, her tortoiseshell cat. Tom was a beauty, and knew his power; he ruled Miss Petingill with a rod of iron, and always sat in the rocking-chair when there was one. It was no matter where *she* sat, Miss Petingill told people, but Tom was delicate, and must be made comfortable. A big family Bible always came too, and a special red merino pin-cushion, and some "shade pictures" of old Mr. and Mrs. Petingill and Peter Petingill, who was drowned at sea; and photographs of Mrs. Porter, who used to be Marcia Petingill, and Mrs. Porter's husband, and all the Porter children. Many little boxes and jars came also, and a long row of phials and bottles, filled with home-made physic and herb teas. Miss Petingill could not have slept without having them beside her, for, as she said, how did she know that she might not be "took sudden" with something, and die for want of a little ginger-balsam or pennyroyal?

The Carr children always made so much noise, that it required something unusual to make Miss Petingill drop her work, as she did now, and fly to the window. In fact there *was* a tremendous hubbub: hurrahs from Dorry, stamping of feet, and a great outcry of shrill, glad voices. Looking down, Miss Petingill saw the whole six—no, seven, for Cecy was there too—stream out of the wood-house door—which wasn't a door, but only a tall open arch—and rush noisily across the yard. Katy was at the head, bearing a large black bottle without any cork in it, while the others carried in each hand what seemed to be a cookie.

"Katherine Carr! Kather-*ine*!" screamed Miss Petingill, tapping loudly on the glass. "Don't you see that it's raining? You ought to be ashamed to let your little brothers and sisters go out and get wet in such a way!" But nobody heard her, and the children vanished into the shed, where nothing could be seen but a distant flapping of pantalettes and frilled trousers, going up what seemed to be a ladder, farther back in the shed. So, with a dissatisfied cluck, Miss Petingill drew back her head, perched the spectacles on her nose and went to work again on Katy's plaid alpaca, which had two immense zigzag rents across the middle of the front breadth. Katy's frocks, strange to say, always tore exactly in that place!

If Miss Petingill's eyes could have reached a little farther, they would have seen that it wasn't a ladder up which the children were climbing, but a tall wooden post, with spikes driven into it about a foot apart. It required quite a stride to get from one spike to the other; in fact, the little ones couldn't have managed it at all, had it not been for Clover and Cecy pushing very hard from below, while Katy, making a long arm, pulled from above. At last they were all safely up, and in the delightful retreat which I am about to describe:

Imagine a low, dark loft without any windows, and

with only a very little light coming in through the square hole in the floor, to which the spiky post led. There was a strong smell of corncobs, though the corn had been taken away; a great deal of dust and spiderweb in the corners, and some wet spots on the boards; for the roof always leaked a little in rainy weather.

This was the place which, for some reason I have never been able to find out, the Carr children preferred to any other on rainy Saturdays, when they could not play out of doors. Aunt Izzie was as much puzzled at this fancy as I am. When she was young (a vague, far-off time, which none of her nieces and nephews believed in much), she had never had any of these queer notions about getting off into holes and corners and poke-away places: Aunt Izzie would gladly have forbidden them to go to the loft, but Dr. Carr had given his permission, so all she could do was to invent stories about children who had broken their bones, in various dreadful ways, by climbing posts and ladders. But these stories made no impression on any of the children except little Phil, and the self-willed brood kept on their way, and climbed their spiked post as often as they liked.

"What's in the bottle?" demanded Dorry, the minute he was fairly landed in the loft.

"Don't be greedy," replied Katy, severely; "you will know when the time comes. It is something *delicious*, I can assure you."

"Now," she went on, having thus quenched Dorry, "all of you had better give me your cookies to put away; if you don't, they'll be sure to be eaten up before the feast, and then, you know, there wouldn't be anything to make a feast of."

So all of them handed over their cookies. Dorry, who had begun on his as he came up the ladder, was a little unwilling, but he was too much in the habit of minding Katy to dare to disobey. The big bottle was set in a corner, and a stack of cookies built up around it.

"That's right," proceeded Katy, who, as oldest and biggest, always took the lead in their plays. "Now, if we're fixed and ready to begin, the Fête [Katy pronounced it *Feet*] can commence. The opening exercise will be 'A Tragedy of the Alhambra', by Miss Hall."

"No," cried Clover; "first 'The Blue Wizard, or Edwitha of the Hebrides', you know, Katy."

"Didn't I tell you?" said Katy; "a dreadful accident has happened to that."

"Oh, what?" cried all the rest, for "Edwitha" was rather a favourite with the family. It was one of the many serial stories which Katy was for ever writing, and was about a lady, a knight, a blue wizard, and a poodle named Bop. It had been going on so many months now that everybody had forgotten the beginning, and nobody had any particular hope of living to hear the end, but still the news of its untimely fate was a shock.

"I'll tell you," said Katy. "Old Judge Kirby called this morning to see Aunt Izzie. I was studying in the little room, but I saw him come in, and pull out the big chair and sit down, and I almost screamed out 'Don't!' "

"Why?" cried the children.

"Don't you see? I had stuffed 'Edwitha' down between the back and the seat. It was a *beau*tiful hiding-place, for the seat goes back ever so far; but 'Edwitha' was such a fat bundle, and old Judge Kirby takes up so much room, that I was afraid there would be trouble. And sure enough, he had hardly dropped down before there was a great crackling of paper, and he jumped up again and called out, 'Bless me! what is that?' And then be began poking and poking, and just as he had poked

48

out the whole bundle, and was putting on his spectacles to see what it was, Aunt Izzie came in."

"Well, what next?" cried the children, immensely tickled.

"Oh!" continued Katy, "Aunt Izzie put on her glasses too, and screwed up her eyes—you know the way she does—and she and the judge read a little bit of it; that part at the first, you remember, where Bop steals the blue pills, and the Wizard tries to throw him into the sea. You can't think how funny it was to hear Aunt Izzie reading 'Edwitha' out aloud—" and Katy went into convulsions at the recollection. "When she got to 'Oh, Bop—my angel Bop!' I just rolled under the table, and stuffed the table-cover in my mouth to keep from screaming right out. By and by I heard her call Debby, and give her the papers, and say, 'Here is a mass of trash which I wish you to put at once into the kitchen fire'. And she told me afterwards that she thought I would be in an insane asylum before I was twenty. It was too bad," ended Katy, half laughing and half crying, "to burn up the new chapter and all. But there's one good thing—she didn't find 'The Fairy of the Dry Goods Box', that was stuffed farther back in the seat.

"And now," continued the mistress of ceremonies, "we will begin. Miss Hall will please rise."

"Miss Hall," much flustered at her fine name, got up with very red cheeks.

"It was once upon a time," she read, "moonlight lay on the halls of the Alhambra, and the knight, striding impatiently down the passage, thought she would never come."

"Who—the moon?" asked Clover.

"No, of course not," replied Cecy; "a lady he was in love with. The next verse is going to tell about her, only you interrupted."

"She wore a turban of silver, with a jewelled crescent. As she stole down the corregidor the beams struck it and it glittered like stars."

" 'So you are come, Zuleika?'

" 'Yes, my lord.'

"Just then a sound as of steel smote upon the ear, and Zuleika's mail-clad father rushed in. He drew his sword, so did the other. A moment more, and they both lay dead and stiff in the beams of the moon. Zuleika gave a loud shriek, and threw herself upon their bodies. She was dead too! And so ends 'The Tragedy of the Alhambra'."

"That's lovely," said Katy, drawing a long breath, "only very sad. What beautiful stories you do write, Cecy! But I wish you wouldn't always kill the people. Why couldn't the knight have killed the father, and—no, I suppose Zuleika wouldn't have married him then. Well, the father might have—oh, bother! why must anybody be killed at all? Why not have them fall on each other's necks, and make up?"

"Why, Katy!" cried Cecy, "it wouldn't have been a tragedy then. You know the name was 'A *Tragedy* of the Alhambra'."

"Oh well," said Katy hurriedly, for Cecy's lips were beginning to pout, and her fair, pinkish face to redden, as if she were about to cry, "perhaps it *was* prettier to have them all die; only your ladies and gentlemen always do die. and I thought, for a change, you know!—What a lovely word that was—'corregidor'—what does it mean?"

"I don't know," replied Cecy, quite consoled. "It was in the 'Conquest of Granada'. Something to walk over. I believe."

"The next," went on Katy, consulting her paper, "is 'Yap, a Simple Poem', by Clover Carr."

All the children giggled, but Clover got up composedly and recited the following verses:

"Did you ever know Yap?
   The best little dog
Who e'er sat on lap
   Or barked at a frog.

"His eyes were like beads,
   His tail like a mop,
And it waggled as if
   It never would stop.

"His hair was like silk
   Of the glossiest sheen,
He always ate milk,
   And once the cold-cream.

"Off the nursery bureau—
   (That line is too long!)
It made him quite ill,
   So endeth my song.

"For Yappy he died
   Just two months ago,
And we oughtn't to sing
   At a funeral, you know."

The "Poem" met with immense applause all the children laughed, and shouted, and clapped, till the loft rang again. But Clover kept her face perfectly, and sat down as demure as ever, except that the little dimples came and went at the corners of her mouth; dimples, partly natural, and partly, I regret to say, the result of a pointed slate pencil, with which Clover was in the habit of deepening them every day while she studied her lessons.

"Now", said Katy, after the noise had subsided, "now comes 'Scripture Verses', by Miss Elsie and Joanna Carr. Hold up your head, Elsie, and speak distinctly; and oh, Johnnie, you *mustn't* giggle in that way when it comes your turn!"

But Johnnie only giggled the harder at this appeal, keeping her hands very tight across her mouth, and peeping out over her fingers. Elsie, however, was solemn as a little judge, and with great dignity began:

> "An angel with a fiery sword,
> Came to send Adam and Eve abroad;
> And as they journeyed through the skies
> They took one look at Paradise.
> "They thought of all the happy hours
> Among the birds and fragrant bowers,
> And Eve she wept, and Adam bawled,
> And both together loudly squalled."

Dorry snickered at this, but sedate Clover hushed him.

"You mustn't," she said; "it's about the Bible, you know. Now, John, it's your turn."

But Johnnie would persist in holding her hands over her mouth, while her fat little shoulders shook with laughter. At last, with a great effort, she pulled her face straight, and speaking as fast as she possibly could, repeated, in a sort of burst:

> "Balaam's donkey saw the Angel
>   And stopped short in fear.
> Balaam didn't see the Angel,
>   Which is very queer."

After which she took refuge again behind her fingers, while Elsie went on:

> "Elijah by the creek,
>   He by ravens fed,
> Took from their horny beak
>   Pieces of meat and bread."

"Come, Johnnie," said Katy, but the incorrigible Johnnie was shaking again, and all they could make out was:

> "The bears came down, and ate—and ate—"

These "Verses" were part of a grand project on which Clover and Elsie had been busy for more than a year. It was a sort of rearrangement of Scripture for infant minds; and when it was finished they meant to have it published, bound in red, with daguerreotypes of the two authoresses on the cover. "The Youth's Poetical Bible" was to be the name of it. Papa, much tickled with the scraps which he overheard, proposed, instead, "The Trundle-Bed Book", as having been composed principally in that spot, but Elsie and Clover were highly indignant, and would not listen to the idea for a moment.

After the "Scripture Verses" came Dorry's turn. He had been allowed to choose for himself, which was unlucky, as his taste was peculiar, not to say gloomy. On this occasion he had selected that cheerful hymn which begins:

> "Hark, from the tombs a doleful sound."

And he now began to recite it in a lugubrious voice and with great emphasis, smacking his lips, as it were, over such lines as:

"Princes, this clay *shall* be your bed,
      In spite of all your towers."

The older children listened with a sort of fascinated horror, rather enjoying the cold chills which ran down their backs, and huddling close together, as Dorry's hollow tones echoed from the dark corners of the loft. It was too much for Philly, however. At the close of the piece he was found to be in tears.

"I don't want to st-a-a-y up here and be groaned at," he sobbed.

"There, you bad boy" cried Katy, all the more angry because she was conscious of having enjoyed it herself, "that's what you do with your horrid hymns, frightening us to death and making Phil cry!" And she gave Dorry a little shake. He began to whimper, and as Phil was still sobbing, and Johnnie had begun to sob too, out of sympathy with the others, the *Feet* in the loft seemed likely to come to a sad end.

"I'm going to tell Aunt Izzie that I don't like you," declared Dorry, putting one leg through the opening in the floor.

"No, you aren't," said Katy, seizing him; "you are going to stay, because *now* we are going to have the Feast! Do stop, Phil; and Johnnie, don't be a goose, but come and pass round the cookies."

The word "Feast" produced a speedy effect on the spirits of the party. Phil cheered at once, and Dorry changed his mind about going. The black bottle was solemnly set in the midst, and the cookies were handed about by Johnnie, who was now all smiles. The cookies had scalloped edges and caraway seeds inside, and were very nice. There were two apiece; and as the last was finished, Katy put her hand in her pocket, and, amid great applause, produced the crowning addition to the repast—seven long, brown sticks of cinnamon.

"Isn't it fun?" she said. "Debby was very good-natured today, and let me put my own hand into the box, so I picked out the longest sticks there were. Now, Cecy, as you're company, you shall have the first drink out of the bottle."

The "something delicious" proved to be weak vinegar-and-water. It was quite warm, but somehow, drunk up there in the loft, and out of a bottle, it tasted very nice. Beside, they didn't *call* it vinegar-and-water—of course not! Each child gave his or her swallow a different name, as if the bottle were like Signor Blitz's and could pour out a dozen things at once. Clover called her share "Raspberry Shrub", Dorry christened his "Ginger Pop", while Cecy, who was romantic, took her three sips under the name of "Hydomel", which she explained was something nice, made, she believed, of beeswax. The last drop gone, and the last bit of cinnamon crunched, the company came to order again, for the purpose of hearing Philly repeat his one piece:

"Little drops of water",

which exciting poem he had said every Saturday as far back as they could remember. After that Katy declared the literary part of the "Feet" over, and they all fell to playing "Stagecoach", which, in spite of close quarters and an occasional bump from the roof, was such good fun that a general "Oh, dear!" welcomed the ringing of the tea-bell. I suppose cookies and vinegar had taken away their appetites, for none of them were hungry, and Dorry astonished Aunt Izzie very much by eyeing the table in a disgusted way, and saying: "Pshaw! *Only*

55

plum sweetmeats and sponge cake and hot biscuit! I don't want any supper."

"What ails the child? He must be sick," said Dr. Carr; but Katy explained:

"Oh no, Papa, it isn't that—only we've been having a feast in the loft."

"Did you have a good time?" asked Papa, while Aunt Izzie gave a dissatisfied groan. And all the children answered at once: "Splendiferous!"

CHAPTER SIX

INTIMATE FRIENDS

"Aunt Izzie, may I ask Imogen Clark to spend the day here on Saturday?" cried Katy, bursting in one afternoon.

"Who on earth is Imogen Clark? I never heard the name before," replied her aunt.

"O, the *loveliest* girl! She has been going to Mrs. Knight's school only a little while, but we're the greatest friends. And she's perfectly beautiful, Aunt Izzie. Her hands are just as white as snow, and no bigger than *that.* She's got the littlest waist of any girl in school, and she's so sweet, and so self-denying and unselfish! I don't believe she has any good times at home, either. Do-let me ask her!"

"How do you know she's so sweet and self-denying, if you've known her such a short time?" asked Aunt Izzie, in an unpromising tone.

"Oh, she tells me everything! We always walk together at recess now. I know all about her, and she's just lovely! Her father used to be very rich, but they're poor now, and Imogen had to have her boots patched twice last winter. I think she's the flower of her family. You can't think how I love her!" concluded Katy, sentimentally.

"No, I can't," said Aunt Izzie. "I never could see into these sudden friendships of yours, Katy, and I'd rather you wouldn't invite this Imogen, or whatever her name is, till I've had a chance to ask somebody about her."

Katy clasped her hands in despair. "Oh, Aunt Izzie!" she cried, "Imogen knows that I came in to ask you, and she's standing at the gate at this moment, waiting to hear what you say. Please let me, just this once! I shall be so dreadfully ashamed not to."

"Well," said Miss Izzie, moved by the wretchedness of Katy's face, "if you've asked her already, it's no use my saying no, I suppose. But recollect, Katy, this is not to happen again. I can't have you inviting girls, and then coming for my leave. Your father won't be at all pleased. He's very particular about whom you make friends with. Remember how Mrs. Spenser turned out."

Poor Katy! Her propensity to fall violently in love with new people was always getting her into scrapes. Ever since she began to walk and talk, "Katy's intimate friends" had been one of the jokes of the household.

Papa once undertook to keep a list of them, but the number grew so great that he gave it up in despair. First on the list was a small Irish child, named Marianne O'Riley. Marianne lived in a street which Katy passed on her way to school. It was not Mrs. Knight's, but an A B C school, to which Dorry and John now went. Marianne used to be always making sand-pies in front

57

of her mother's house, and Katy, who was about five years old, often stopped to help her. Over this mutual pastry they grew so intimate, that Katy resolved to adopt Marianne as her own little girl, and bring her up in a safe and hidden corner.

She told Clover of this plan, but nobody else. The two children, full of their delightful secret, began to save pieces of bread and cookies from their supper every evening. By degrees they collected a great heap of dry crusts, and other refreshments, which they put safely away in the garret. They also saved the apples which were given them for two weeks,-and made a bed in a big empty box, with cotton quilts, and the dolls' pillows out of the baby-house. When all was ready, Katy broke the plan to her beloved Marianne, and easily persuaded her to run away and take possession of this new home.

"We won't tell Papa and Mamma till she's quite grown up," Katy said to Clover; "then we'll bring her downstairs, and *won't* they be surprised? Don't let's call her Marianne any longer, either. It isn't pretty. We'll name her Susquehanna instead—Susquehanna Carr. Recollect, Marianne, you mustn't answer if I call you Marianne—only when I say Susquehanna."

"Yes'm," replied Marianne very meekly.

For a whole day all went on delightfully. Susquehanna lived in her wooden box, ate all the apples and the freshest cookies, and was happy. The two children took turns to steal away and play with the "baby", as they called Marianne, though she was a great deal bigger than Clover. But when night came on, and nurse swooped on Katy and Clover, and carried them off to bed, Miss O'Riley began to think that the garret was a dreadful place. Peeping out of her box, she could see black things standing in corners, which she did not recollect seeing in the day time. They were really trunks and brooms and warming-pans, but somehow, in the darkness, they looked different—big and awful. Poor little Marianne bore it as long as she could; but when at last a rat began to scratch in the wall close beside her, her courage gave way entirely, and she screamed at the top of her voice.

"What is that?" said Dr. Carr, who had just come in, and was on his way upstairs.

"It sounds as if it came from the attic," said Mrs. Carr (for this was before Mamma died). "Can it be that one of the children has got out of bed and wandered upstairs in her sleep?"

No, Katy and Clover were safe in the nursery, so Dr. Carr took a candle and went as fast as he could to the attic, where the yells were growing terrific. When he reached the top of the stairs, the cries ceased. He looked about. Nothing was to be seen at first, then a little head appeared over the edge of a-big wooden box, and a piteous voice sobbed out:

"Ah, Miss Katy, and indeed I can't be stayin' any longer. There's rats in it!"

"Who on earth are *you*?" asked the amazed Doctor.

"Sure I'm Miss Katy's and Miss Clover's baby. But I don't want to be a baby any longer. I want to go home and see my mother." And again the poor little midge lifted up her voice and wept.

I don't think Dr. Carr ever laughed so hard in his life, as when finally he got to the bottom of the story, and found that Katy and Clover had been "adopting" a child. But he was very kind to poor Susquehanna, and carried her downstairs in his arms, to the nursery. There, in a bed close to the other children, she soon forgot her troubles and fell asleep.

The little sisters were much surprised when they

awoke in the morning, and found their baby asleep beside them. But their joy was speedily turned to tears. After breakfast, Dr. Carr carried Marianne home to her mother, who was in a great fright over her disappearance, and explained to the children that the garret plan must be given up. Great was the mourning in the nursery; but as Marianne was allowed to come and play with them now and then, they gradually got over their grief. A few months later Mr. O'Riley moved away from Burnet, and that was the end of Katy's first friendship.

The next was even funnier. There was a queer old black woman who lived all alone by herself in a small house near the school. This old woman had a very bad temper. The neighbours told horrible stories about her, so that the children were afraid to pass the house. They used to turn always just before they reached it, and cross to the other side of the street. This they did so regularly that their feet had worn a path in the grass. But for some reason Katy found a great fascination in the little house. She liked to dodge about the door, always holding herself ready to turn and run in case the old woman rushed out upon her with a broomstick. One day she begged a large cabbage of Alexander, and rolled it in at the door of the house. The old woman seemed to like it, and after this Katy always stopped to speak when she went by. She even got so far as to sit on the step and watch the old woman at work. There was a sort of perilous pleasure in doing this. It was like sitting at the entrance of a lion's cage, uncertain at what moment his Majesty might take it into his head to give a spring and eat you up.

After this, Katy took a fancy to a couple of twin sisters, daughters of a German jeweller. They were quite grown-up and always wore dresses exactly alike.

Hardly anyone could tell them apart. They spoke very little English, and as Katy didn't know a word of German, their intercourse was confined to smiles, and to the giving of bunches of flowers, which Katy used to tie up and present to them whenever they passed the gate. She was too shy to do more than just put the flowers in their hands-and run away; but the twins were evidently pleased, for one day, when Clover happened to be looking out of the window, she saw them open the gate, fasten a little parcel to a bush, and walk rapidly off. Of course she called Katy at once, and the two children flew out to see what the parcel was. It held a bonnet—a beautiful doll's bonnet of blue silk, trimmed with artificial flowers; upon it was pinned a slip of paper with these words, in an odd foreign hand:

"To the nice little girl who was so kindly to give us some flowers."

You can judge whether Katy and Clover were pleased or not.

This was when Katy was six years old. I can't begin to tell you how many different friends she had set up since then. There was an ash-man and a steam-boat captain. There was Mrs. Sawyer's cook, a nice old woman, who gave Katy lessons in cooking, and taught her to make soft custard and sponge cake. There was a bonnet-maker, pretty and dressy, whom, to Aunt Izzie's great indignation, Katy persisted in calling "Cousin Estelle"! There was a thief in the town-jail, under whose window Katy used to stand saying, "I'm so sorry, poor man!" and "Have you got any little girls like me?" in the most piteous way. The thief had a piece of string which he let down from the window. Katy would tie rosebuds and cherries to this string, and the thief would draw them up. It was so interesting to do this, that Katy felt dreadful when they carried the man off to the State Prison. Then followed a short interval of Cornelia Perham, a nice, good-natured girl, whose father was a fruit merchant. I am afraid Katy's liking for prunes and white grapes played a part in this intimacy. It was splendid fun to go with Cornelia to her father's big shop, and have whole boxes of raisins and drums of figs opened for their amusement, and be allowed to ride up and down in the elevator as much as they liked. But of all Katy's queer acquaintances, Mrs.Spenser, to whom Aunt Izzie had alluded, was the queerest.

Mrs.Spenser was a mysterious lady whom nobody ever saw. Her husband was a handsome, rather bad-looking man, who had come from parts unknown, and rented a small house in Burnet. He didn't seem to have any particular business, and was away from home a great deal. His wife was said to be an invalid, and people, when they spoke of him, shook their heads and wondered how the poor woman got on all alone in the house, while her husband was absent.

Of course, Katy was too young to understand these whispers, or the reasons why people were not disposed to think well of Mr. Spenser. The romance of the closed door and the lady whom nobody saw interested her very much. She used to stop and stare at the windows, and wonder what was going on inside, till at last it seemed as if she *must* know. So one day she took some flowers and Victoria, her favourite doll, and boldly marched into Spenser's yard.

She tapped at the front door, but nobody answered. Then she tapped again. Still nobody answered. She tried the door. It was locked. So, shouldering Victoria, she trudged round to the back of the house. As she passed the side-door, she saw that it was open a little way. She knocked for the third time, and as no one came, she went in, and passing through the little hall began to tap at all the inside doors.

There seemed to be no people in the house. Katy peeped into the kitchen first. It was bare and forlorn. All sorts of dishes were standing about. There was no fire in the stove. The parlour was not much better. Mr. Spenser's boots lay in the middle of the floor. There were dirty glasses on the table. On the mantelpiece was a platter with bones of meat upon it. Dust lay thick over everything, and the whole house looked as if it hadn't been lived in for at least a year.

Katy tried several other doors, all of which were locked, and then she went upstairs. As she stood on the top step, grasping her flowers, and a little doubtful what to do next, a feeble voice from a bedroom called out:

"Who is there?"

This was Mrs. Spenser. She was lying on her bed, which was very tossed and tumbled, as if it hadn't been made up that morning. The room was as disorderly and dirty as all the rest of the house, and Mrs. Spenser's wrapper and night-cap were by no means clean, but her face was sweet, and she had beautiful curling hair, which fell over the pillow. She was evidently very ill, and altogether Katy felt sorrier for her than she had ever done for anybody in her life.

"Who are you, child?" asked Mrs. Spenser.

"I'm Dr. Carr's little girl," answered Katy, going straight up to the bed. "I came to bring you some flowers." And she laid the bouquet on the dirty sheet.

Mrs. Spenser seemed to like the flowers. She took them up and smelled them for a long time, without speaking.

"But how did you get in?" she said at last.

"The door was open," faltered Katy, who was beginning to feel scared at her own daring, "and they said you were ill, so I thought perhaps you would like me to come and see you."

"You are a kind little girl," said Mrs. Spenser, and gave her a kiss.

After this Katy used to go every day. Sometimes Mrs. Spenser would be up and moving feebly about; but more often she was in bed, and Katy would sit beside her. The house never looked a bit better than it did that first day, but after a while Katy used to brush Mrs. Spenser's hair, and wash her face with the corner of a towel.

I think her visits were a comfort to the poor lady, who was very ill and lonely. Sometimes, when she felt pretty well, she would tell Katy stories about the time when *she* was a little girl and lived at home with her father and mother. But she never spoke of Mr. Spenser, and Katy never saw him except once, when she was so frightened that for several days she dared not go near the house. At last Cecy reported that she had seen him go off in the stage with his carpet-bag, so Katy ventured in again. Mrs Spenser cried when she saw her.

"I thought you were never coming any more," she said.

Katy was touched and flattered at having been missed, and after that she never lost a day. She always carried the prettiest flowers she could find, and if anyone gave her a specially nice peach or a bunch of grapes she saved it for Mrs. Spenser.

Aunt Izzie was much worried at all this, But Dr Carr would not interfere. He said it was a case where grown people could do nothing, and if Katy was a comfort to the poor lady he was glad. Katy was glad too, and the visits did her as much good as they did Mrs. Spenser, for the intense pity she felt for the sick woman made her gentle and patient as she had never been before.

One day she stopped, as usual, on her way home from school. She tried the side door—it was locked; the back door—it was locked too. All the blinds were shut tight. This was very puzzling.

As she stood in the yard a woman put her head out of the window of the next house. "It's no use knocking," she said, "all the folks have gone away."

"Gone away where?" asked Katy.

"Nobody knows," said the woman; "the gentleman came back in the middle of the night, and this morning, before light, he had a wagon at the door, and just put in the trunks and the sick lady, and drove off. There's been more than one a-knocking besides you, since then. But Mr. Pudgett, he's got the key, and nobody can get in without going to him."

It was too true Mrs. Spenser was gone, and Katy never saw her again. In a few days it came out that Mr. Spenser was a very bad man, and had been making false money—*counterfeiting*, as grown up people call it. The police were searching for him to put him in jail, and that was the reason he had come back in such a hurry and carried off his poor sick wife. Aunt Izzie cried with mortification when she heard this. She said she thought it was a disgrace that Katy should have been visiting in a counterfeiter's family. But Dr. Carr only laughed. He told Aunt Izzie that he didn't think that kind of crime was catching, and as for Mrs. Spenser, she was much to be pitied. But Aunt Izzie could not get over her vexation, and every now and then, when she was vexed, she would refer to the affair; though this all happened so long ago that most people had forgotten all about it, and Philly and John

65

had stopped playing at "Putting Mr. Spenser in Jail", which for a long time was one of their favourite games.

Katy always felt badly when Aunt Izzie spoke unkindly of her poor sick friend. She had tears in her eyes now, as she walked to the gate, and looked so very sober, that Imogen Clark, who stood there waiting, clasped her hands and said:

"Ah, I see! Your aristocratic aunt refuses."

Imogen's real name was Elizabeth. She was rather a pretty girl, with a screwed-up, sentimental mouth, shiny brown hair, and a little round curl on each of her cheeks. These curls must have been fastened on with glue or tintacks', one would think, for they never moved. however much she laughed or shook her head. Imogen was a bright girl. naturally, but she had read so many novels that her brain was completely turned. It was partly this which made her so attractive to Katy, who adored stories, and thought Imogen was a real heroine of romance.

"Oh no, she doesn't," she relplied, hardly able to keep from laughing, at the idea of Aunt Lizzie being called an "aristocratic" relative—"she says she shall be very hap—" But here Katy's conscience gave a prick, and the sentence ended in "um, um, um—" "So you'll come won't you, darling? I am so glad!"

"And I!" said Imogen, turning up her eyes theatrically.

From this time on till the end of the weekthe children talked of nothing but Imogen's visit and the nice time they were going to have. Before breakfast on Saturday morning, Katy and Clover were at work building a beautiful bower of asparagus boughs under the trees. All the playthings were set out in order. Debby baked them some cinnamon cakes, the kitten had a pink ribbon tied round her neck, and the dolls, including "Pipery", were arrayed in their best clothes.

About half-past ten Imogen arrived. She was dressed in a light-blue *barège*, with low neck and short sleeves, and wore coral beads in her hair, white satin slippers and a pair of yellow gloves. The gloves and slippers were quite dirty, and the *barège* was old and darned; but the general effect was so very gorgeous, that the children, who were dressed for play, in gingham frocks and white aprons, were quite dazzled at the appearance of their guest.

"Oh, Imogen, you look just like a young lady in a story!" said simple Katy; whereupon Imogen tossed her head, and rustled her skirts about more than ever.

Somehow, with these fine clothes. Imogen seemed to have put on a fine manner, quite different from the one she used every day. You know some people always do. when they go out visiting. You would almost have supposed that this was a different Imogen, who was kept in a box most of the time, and taken out for Sundays and grand occasions. She pirouetted about, and simpered and lisped. and looked at herself in the glass, and as generally grown-up and airy. When Aunt Izzie spoke to her. she fluttered and behaved so queerly, that Clover almost laughed; and even Katy, who could see nothing wrong in people she loved, was glad to carry her away to the playroom.

"Come out to the bower," she said, putting her arm round the blue *barège* waist.

"A bower!" cried Imogen. "How sweet!" But when they reached the asparagus boughs her face fell. "Why, it hasn't any roof, or pinnacles, or any fountain!" she said.

"Why, no, of course not," said Clover, staring; "we made it ourselves."

"Oh!" said Imogen. She was evidently disappointed. Katy and Clover felt mortified; but as their visitor did not care for the bower, they tried to think of something else.

"Let us go to the loft," they said.

So they all crossed the yard together. Imogen picked her way daintily in the white satin slippers but when she saw the spiked post, she gave a scream.

"Oh, not up there, darling, not up there!" she cried. "Never, never!"

"Oh, do try! It's just as easy as can be," pleaded Katy, going up and down half a dozen times in succession to show how easy it was. But Imogen wouldn't be persuaded.

"Do not ask me," she said affectedly; "my nerves would never stand such a thing! And besides—my dress!"

"What made you wear it?" said Philly, who was a plainspoken child, and given to questions. While John whispered to Dorry. "That's a very stupid girl. Let's go off somewhere and play by ourselves."

So, one by one, the small fry crept away, leaving Katy and Clover to entertain the visitor by themselves. They tried dolls, but Imogen did not care for dolls. Then they proposed to sit down in the shade, and cap verses. a game they all liked. But Imogen said that though she adored poetry, she never could remember any. So it ended in their going to the orchard, where Imogen ate a great many plums and early apples, and really seemed to enjoy herself. But when she could eat no more, a dreadful dullness fell over the party. At last Imogen said:

"Don't you ever sit in the drawing-room?"

"The what?" asked Clover.

"The drawing-room," repeated Imogen.

"Oh, she means the parlour!" cried Katy. "No, we don't sit there except when Aunt Izzie has company to tea. It is all dark and poky, you know. Besides, it's so much pleasanter to be outdoors. Don't you think so?"

"Yes, sometimes," replied Imogen, doubtfully; "but I think it would be pleasant to go and sit there for a while, now. My head aches dreadfully, being out here in this horrid sun."

Katy was at her wits' end to know what to do. They scarcely ever went into the parlour, which Aunt Izzie regarded as a sort of sacred place. She kept cotton petticoats over all the chairs for fear of dust, and never opened the blinds for fear of flies. The idea of children with dusty boots going in there to sit! On the other hand, Katy's natural politeness made it hard to refuse a visitor anything she asked for. And besides, it was dreadful to think that Imogen might go away and report "Katy Carr isn't allowed to sit in the best room, even when she has company!" With a quaking heart she led the way to the parlour. She dared not open the blinds, so the room looked very dark. She could just see Imogen's figure as she sat on the sofa, and Clover twirling uneasily about on the piano-stool. All the time she kept listening to hear if Aunt Izzie were not coming; and altogether the parlour was a dismal place to her, not half so pleasant as the asparagus bower, where they felt perfectly safe.

But Imogen, who for the first time seemed comfortable, began to talk. Her talk was about herself. Such stories she told about the things which had happened to her! All the young ladies in The Ledger put together never had stranger adventures. Gradually Katy and Clover got so interested that they left their seats and crouched down close to the sofa, listening with open mouths to these stories. Katy forgot to listen for Aunt

Izzie. The parlour door swung open, but she did not notice it. She did not even hear the front door shut, when Papa came home to dinner.

Dr. Carr, stopping in the hall to glance over his newspaper, heard the high-pitched voice running on in the parlour. At first he hardly listened; then these words caught his ear:

"Oh, it was lovely, girls, perfectly delicious! I suppose I did look well, for I was all in white, with my hair let down, and just one rose, you know, here on the top. And he leaned over me, and said in a low, deep tone, 'Lady, I am a brigand, but I feel the enchanting power of beauty. You are free!'"

Dr. Carr pushed the door open a little farther. Nothing was to be seen but some indistinct figures, but he heard Katy's voice in an eager tone:

"Oh, *do* go on. What happened next?"

"Who on earth have the children got in the parlour?" he asked Aunt Izzie, whom he found in the dining-room.

"The parlour!" cried Miss Izzie wrathfully. "Why, what are they there for?" Then, going to the door, she called out, "Children, what are you doing in the parlour? Come out at once. I thought you were playing outdoors."

"Imogen had a headache," faltered Katy. The three girls came out into the hall; Clover and Katy looking scared, and even the enchanter of the brigand quite crestfallen.

"Oh," said Aunt Izzie grimly, "I am sorry to hear that. Probably you are bilious. Would you like some camphor or anything?"

"No, thank you," replied Imogen meekly. But afterwards she whispered to Katy: "Your aunt isn't very nice, I think. She's just like Jackima, that horrid old woman I told you about, who lived in the Brigand's Cave, and did the cooking."

70

"I don't think you are a bit polite to tell me so," retorted Katy, very angry at this speech.

"Oh, never mind, dear; don't take it to heart!" replied Imogen sweetly. "We can't help having relations that are not nice, you know." The visit was evidently not a success. Papa was very civil to Imogen at dinner, but he watched her closely, and Katy saw a comical twinkle in his eye, which she did not like. Papa had very droll eyes. They saw everything, and sometimes they seemed to talk almost as distinctly as his tongue. Katy began to feel low-spirited. She confessed afterward that she should never have got through the afternoon if she hadn't run upstairs two or three times and comforted herself by reading a little in "Rosamond".

"Aren't you glad she's gone?" whispered Clover, as they stood at the gate together watching Imogen walk down the street.

"Oh, Clover! How can you?" said Katy. But she gave Clover a great hug, and I think in her heart she *was* glad.

"Katy," said Papa next day, "you came into the room then, exactly like your new friend Miss Clark."

"How? I don't know what you mean," answered Katy, blushing deeply.

"*So*", said Dr. Carr; and he got up, raising his shoulders and squaring his elbows; and took a few mincing steps across the room. Katy couldn't help laughing, it was so funny, and so like Imogen. Then Papa sat down again and drew her close to him.

"My dear," he said, "you're an affectionate child, and I'm glad of it. But there is such a thing as throwing away one's affection. I didn't fancy that little girl at all yesterday. What makes you like her so much?"

"I didn't like her so much yesterday," admitted Katy,

reluctantly. "She's a great deal nicer than that at school, sometimes."

"I'm glad to hear it," said her father. "For I should be sorry to think that you really admired such silly manners. And what was that nonsense I heard her telling you about brigands?"

"It really hap—" began Katy. Then she caught Papa's eye, and bit her lip, for he looked very quizzical. "Well," she went on, laughing, "I suppose it didn't really all happen; but it was ever so funny, Papa, even if it was a make-up. And Imogen's just as good-natured as can be. All the girls like her."

"Make-ups are all very well," said Papa, "as long as people don't try to make you believe they are true. When they do that, it seems to me it comes too near the edge of falsehood to be very safe or pleasant. If I were you, Katy, I'd be a little shy of swearing eternal friendship for Miss Clark. She may be good-natured, as you say, but I think two or three years hence she won't seem so nice to you as she does now. Give me a kiss, chick, and run away, for there's Alexander with the dog-cart."

CHAPTER SEVEN

COUSIN HELEN'S VISIT

A little knot of the schoolgirls were walking home together one afternoon in July. As they neared Dr. Carr's gate, Maria Fiske exclaimed at the sight of a pretty bunch of flowers lying in the middle of the sidewalk:

"Oh my!" she cried. "See what somebody's dropped! I'm going to have it." She stooped to pick it up. But, just as her fingers touched the stems, the nosegay, as if bewitched, began to move. Maria made a bewildered clutch. The nosegay moved faster, and at last vanished under the gate, while a giggle sounded from the other side of the hedge.

"Did you see that?" shrieked Maria. "Those flowers ran away by themselves."

"Nonsense," said Katy, "it's those absurd children." Then, opening the gate, she called: "John! Dorry! Come out and show yourselves." But nobody replied, and no one could be seen. The nosegay lay on the path, however, and picking it up Katy exhibited to the girls a long end of black thread, tied to the stems.

"That's a very favourite trick of Johnnie's," she said; "she and Dorry are always tying up flowers, and putting them out on the walk to tease people. Here, Maria, take them if you like. Though I don't think John's taste in bouquets is very good."

"Isn't it splendid to have vacation come?" said one of the bigger girls. "What are you all going to do? We're going to the seaside."

"Papa says he'll take Susie and me to Niagara," said Maria.

"I'm going to pay my aunt a visit" said Alice Blair. "She lives in a really lovely place in the country. and there's a pond there; and Tom (that's my cousin) says he'll teach me to row. What are you going to do, Katy?"

"Oh, I don't know; play about and have splendid times," replied Katy. throwing her bag of books into the air, and catching it again. But the other girls looked as if they didn't think this good fun at all, and as if they were sorry for her; and Katy felt suddenly that her vacation wasn't going to be so pleasant as that of the rest.

"I wish Papa *would* take us somewhere," she said to Clover, as they walked up the gravel path. "All the other girls' papas do."

"He's too busy," replied Clover. "Besides. I don't think any of the rest of the girls have half such good times as we. Ellen Robbins says she'd give a million dollars for such nice brothers and sisters as ours to play with. And, you know, Maria and Susie have *awful* times at home, though they do go to places. Mrs. Fiske is so particular. She always says 'Don't', and they haven't got any yard to their house, or anything. I wouldn't change."

"Nor I," said Katy, cheering up at these words of wisdom. "Oh, isn't it lovely to think there won't be any school tomorrow? Vacations are just splendid!" and she gave her bag another toss. It fell to the ground with a crash.

"There, you've cracked your slate," said Clover.

"No matter, I shan't want it again for eight weeks," replied Katy comfortably, as they ran up the steps.

They burst open the front door, and raced upstairs crying "Hurrah! hurrah! Vacation's begun! Aunt Izzie, vacation's begun!" Then they stopped short, for lo! the upper hall was all in confusion. Sounds of beating and dusting came from the spare room. Tables and chairs were standing about; and a cot-bed, which seemed to be taking a walk all by itself, had stopped short at the head of the stairs, and barred the way.

"Why, how queer!" said Katy, trying to get past. "What *can* be going to happen? Oh, there's Aunt Izzie! Aunt Izzie, who's coming? What *are* you moving the things out of the Blue Room for?"

"Oh, gracious! Is that you?" replied Aunt Izzie, who looked very hot and flurried. "Now, children, it's no use for you to stand there asking questions; 1 haven't got time to answer them. Let the bedstead alone, Katy, you'll push it into the wall. There, I told you so!" as Katy gave an impatient shove. "You've made a bad mark on the paper. What a troublesome child you are! Go right downstairs, both of you, and don't come up this way again till after tea. I've just as much as I can possibly attend to till then."

"Just tell us what's going to happen, and we will," cried the children.

"Your Cousin Helen is coming to visit us," said Miss Izzie curtly, and disappeared into the Blue Room.

This was news indeed. Katy and Clover ran downstairs in great excitement, and after consulting a little, retired to the loft to talk it over in peace and quiet. Cousin Helen coming! It seemed as strange as if Queen Victoria, gold crown and all, had invited herself to tea. Or as if some character out of a book, Robinson Crusoe, say, or Amy Herbert, had driven up with a trunk, and announced the intention of spending a week. For to the imaginations of the children, Cousin Helen was as interesting and unreal as anybody in the Fairy Tales—Cinderella, or Bluebeard, or dear Red Riding Hood herself. Only there was a sort of mixture of Sunday-school book in their idea of her, for Cousin Helen was very, very good.

None of them had ever seen her. Philly said he was sure she hadn't any legs, because she never went away from home, and lay on a sofa all the time. But the rest knew that this was because Cousin Helen was ill. Papa always went to visit her twice a year, and he liked to talk to the children about her, and tell how sweet and patient she was, and what a pretty room she lived in.

Katy and Clover had "played Cousin Helen" so long, that now they were frightened as well as glad at the idea of seeing the real one.

"Do you suppose she will want us to say hymns to her *all* the time?" asked Clover.

"Not all the time," replied Katy, "because you know she'll get tired, and have to take naps in the afternoons. And then, of course, she reads the Bible a great deal. Oh dear, how quiet we shall have to be! I wonder how long she's going to stay?"

"What do you suppose she looks like?" went on Clover.

"Something like 'Lucy', in Mrs. Sherwood, I suppose, with blue eyes, and curls, and a long, straight nose. And she'll keep her hands clasped *so* all the time, and wear 'frilled wrappers', and lie on the sofa perfectly still, and never smile, but just look patient. We'll have to take off our boots in the hall, Clover, and go upstairs in stocking feet, so as not to make a noise, all the time she stays."

"Won't it be funny!" giggled Clover, her sober little face growing bright at the idea of this variation on the hymns.

The time seemed very long till the next afternoon, when Cousin Helen was expected. Aunt Izzie, who was in a great excitement, gave the children many orders about their behaviour. They were to do this and that, and not to do the other. Dorry at last announced that he wished Cousin Helen would just stay at home. Clover and Elsie, who had been thinking pretty much the same thing in private, were glad to hear that she was on her way to a water-cure, and would stay only four days.

Five o'clock came. They all sat on the steps waiting for the carriage. At last it drove up. Papa was on the box. He motioned the children to stand back. Then he helped out a nice-looking woman, who, Aunt Izzie told them, was Cousin Helen's nurse, and then, very carefully, lifted Cousin Helen in his arms and brought her in.

"Oh, there are the chicks!" were the first words the children heard, in *such* a gay, pleasant voice. "Do set me down somewhere, Uncle. I want to see them so much!"

So Papa put Cousin Helen on the hall sofa. The nurse fetched a pillow, and when she was made comfortable, Dr. Carr called to the little ones.

"Cousin Helen wants to see you," he said.

"Indeed I do," said the bright voice. "So this is Katy? Why, what a splendid tall Katy it is! And this is Clover," kissing her; "and *this* dear little Elsie. You all look as natural as possible—just as if I had seen you before." And she hugged them all round. not as if it was polite to like them because they were relations, but as if she had loved them and wanted them all her life.

There was something in Cousin Helen's face and manner which made the children at home with her at once. Even Philly, who had backed away with his hands behind him, after staring hard for a minute or two, came up with a sort of rush to get his share of kissing.

Still, Katy's first feeling was one of disappointment. Cousin Helen was not at all like "Lucy" in Mrs. Sherwood's story. Her nose turned up the least bit in the world. She had brown hair, which didn't curl, a brown skin, and bright eyes, which danced when she laughed or spoke. Her face was thin, but except for that you wouldn't have guessed that she was sick. She didn't fold her hands, and she didn't look patient, but absolutely glad and merry. Her dress wasn't a "frilled wrapper", but a sort of loose travelling thing of pretty grey stuff, with a rose-coloured bow, and bracelets, and a round hat trimmed with a grey feather. All Katy's dreams about the "saintly invalid" seemed to take wings and fly away. But the more she watched Cousin Helen the more she seemed to like her, and to feel as if she were nicer than the imaginary person which she and Clover had invented.

"She looks just like other people, doesn't she?" whispered Cecy, who had come over to have a peep at the new arrival.

"Y-e-s," replied Katy doubtfully, "only a great, great deal prettier."

By and by, Papa carried Cousin Helen upstairs. All the children wanted to go too, but he told them she was tired, and must rest. So they went outdoors to play till tea time.

"Oh, do let me take up the tray," cried Katy at the tea table, as she watched Aunt Izzie getting ready Cousin Helen's supper. Such a nice supper! Cold chicken, and raspberries and cream, and tea in a pretty pink-and-white china cup. And such a snow-white napkin as Aunt Izzie spread over the tray!

"No, indeed," said Aunt Izzie; "you'll drop it the first thing." But Katy's eyes begged so hard, that Dr. Carr said: "Yes, let her, Izzie; I like to see the girls useful."

So Katy, proud of the commission, took the tray and carried it carefully across the hall. There was a bowl of flowers on the table. As she passed. she was struck with a bright idea. She set down the tray, and picking out a rose, laid it on the napkin beside the saucer of crimson raspberries. It looked very pretty, and Katy smiled to herself with pleasure.

"What are you stopping for?" called Aunt Izzie, from

the dining-room. "*Do* be careful, Katy. I really think Bridget had better take it."

"Oh, no, no!" protested Katy; "I'm almost up already." And she sped upstairs as fast as she could go. Luckless speed! She had just reached the door of the Blue Room, when she tripped upon her bootlace, which, as usual, was dangling, made a mis-step, and stumbled. She caught at the door to save herself; the door flew open; and Katy, with the tray, cream, raspberries, rose and all, descended in a confused heap upon the carpet.

"I told you so!" exclaimed Aunt Izzie from the bottom of the stairs.

Katy never forgot how kind Cousin Helen was on this occasion. She was in bed, and was of course a good deal startled at the sudden crash and tumble on her floor. But after one little jump, nothing could have been sweeter than the way in which she comforted poor crestfallen Katy, and made so merry over the accident, that even Aunt Izzie almost forgot to scold. The broken dishes were piled up and the carpet made clean again, while Aunt Izzie prepared another tray just as nice as the first.

"Please let Katy bring it up!" pleaded Cousin Helen in her pleasant voice. "I am sure she will be careful this time. And Katy, I want just such another rose on the napkin. That was your doing—wasn't it?"

Katy *was* careful; this time all went well. The tray was placed safely on a little table beside the bed, and Katy sat watching Cousin Helen eat her supper with a warm loving feeling at her heart. I think we are scarcely ever so grateful to people as when they help us to get back our own self-esteem.

Cousin Helen hadn't much appetite, though she declared everything was delicious. Katy could see that she was very tired.

"Now," she said, when she had finished, "if you'll shake up this pillow—*so*, and move this other pillow a little, I think I will settle myself to sleep. Thanks— that's just right. Why, Katy dear, you are a born nurse. Now kiss me. Good night! Tomorrow we will have a nice talk."

Katy went downstairs very happy. "Cousin Helen's perfectly lovely," she told Clover. "And she's got on the most *beautiful* nightgown, all lace and rules. It's just like a nightgown in a book."

"Isn't it wicked to care about clothes when you're sick?" questioned Cecy.

"I don't believe Cousin Helen *could* do anything wicked," said Katy.

"I told Mamma that she had on bracelets, and Mamma said she feared your cousin was a worldly person," retorted Cecy, primming up her lips.

Katy and Clover were quite distressed at this opinion. They talked about it while they were undressing.

"I mean to ask Cousin Helen tomorrow," said Katy.

Next morning the children got up very early. They were so glad that it was vacation. If it hadn't been, they would have been forced to go to school without seeing Cousin Helen, for she didn't wake till late. They grew so impatient of the delay, and went upstairs so often to listen at the door, and see if she were moving, that Aunt Izzie finally had to order them off. Katy rebelled against this order a good deal, but she consoled herself by going into the garden and picking the prettiest flowers she could find to give to Cousin Helen the moment she should see her.

When Aunt Izzie let her go up, Cousin Helen was lying on the sofa all dressed for the day in a fresh blue muslin, with blue ribbons, and pretty bronze slippers with rosettes on the toes.

The sofa had been wheeled round with its back to the light. There was a cushion with a pretty fluted cover, that Katy had never seen before, and several other things were scattered about, which gave the room quite a different air. All the house was neat, but somehow Aunt Izzie's rooms never were *pretty*. Children's eyes are quick to perceive such things, and Katy saw at once that the Blue Room had never looked like this.

Cousin Helen was white and tired. but her eyes and smile were as bright as ever. She was delighted with the flowers, which Katy presented rather shyly.

"O, how lovely!" she said; "I must put them in water immediately. Katy dear, won't you bring that little vase on the bureau and set it on this chair beside me? And please pour a little water into it first."

"What a beauty!" cried Katy, as she lifted the graceful white cup swung on a gilt stand. "Is it yours, Cousin Helen?"

"Yes, it is my pet vase. It stands on a little tablet beside me at home, and I fancied that the water-cure would seem more home-like if I had it with me there, so I brought it along. But why do you look so puzzled, Katy? Does it seem queer that a vase should travel about in a trunk?"

"No," said Katy slowly; "I was only thinking— Cousin Helen, is it worldly to have pretty things when you're sick?"

Cousin Helen laughed heartily. "What put that idea into your head?" she asked.

"Cecy said so when I told her about your beautiful nightgown."

Cousin Helen laughed again. "Well," she said, "I'll tell you what I think, Katy. Pretty things are no more 'worldly' than ugly ones, except when they spoil us by

81

making us vain, or careless of the comfort of other people. And sickness is such a disagreeable thing in itself that, unless sick people take great pains, they soon grow to be eyesores to themselves and everybody about them. I don't think it is possible for an invalid to be too particular. And when one has the backache, and the headache, and the all-over-ache," she added, smiling, "there isn't much danger of growing vain because of a rule more or less on one's nightgown or a bit of bright ribbon."

Then she began to arrange the flowers, touching each separate one gently, and as if she loved it.

"What a queer noise!" she exclaimed, suddenly stopping.

It *was* queer—a sort of snarling and snorting sound, as if a walrus or a sea-horse were promenading up and down in the hall. Katy opened the door. Behold! there were John and Dorry, very red in the face from flattening their noses against the keyhole, in a vain attempt to see if Cousin Helen were up and ready to receive company.

"Oh, let them come in!" cried Cousin Helen from her sofa.

So they came in, followed, before long, by Clover and Elsie. Such a merry morning they had! Cousin Helen proved to possess a perfect genius for story-telling, and for suggesting games which could be played about her sofa, and did not make more noise than she could bear. Aunt Izzie, dropping in about eleven o'clock, found them having such a good time that, almost before she knew it, *she* was drawn into the game too. Nobody had ever heard of such a thing before! There sat Aunt Izzie on the floor, with three long lamp-lighters stuck in her hair, playing, "I'm a genteel lady, always genteel," in the jolliest manner possible. The children were so enchanted at the spectacle that they could hardly attend to the game, and were always forgetting how many "horns" they had. Clover privately thought that Cousin Helen must be a witch; and Papa, when he came home at noon, said almost the same thing.

"What have you been doing to them, Helen?" he inquired, as he opened the door and saw the merry circle on the carpet. Aunt Izzie's hair was half pulled down, and Philly was rolling over and over in convulsions of laughter. But Cousin Helen said she hadn't done anything, and pretty soon Papa was on the floor too, playing away as fast as the rest.

"I must put a stop to this," he cried, when everybody was tired of laughing, and everybody's head was stuck as full of paper quills as a porcupine's back. "Cousin Helen will be worn out. Run away, all of you, and don't come near this door again till the clock strikes four. Do you hear, chicks? Run—run! Shoo! shoo!"

The children scuttled away like a brood of fowls— all but Katy. "Oh, Papa, I'll be *so* quiet!" she pleaded. "Mightn't I stay just till the dinner-bell rings?"

"Do let her!" said Cousin Helen. So Papa said, "Yes."

Katy sat on the floor, holding Cousin Helen's hand, and listening to her talk with Papa. It interested her, though it was about things and people she did not know.

"How is Alex?" asked Dr. Carr at length.

"Quite well now," replied Cousin Helen, with one of her brightest looks. "He was run down and tired in the spring, and we were a little anxious about him, but Emma persuaded him to take a fortnight's vacation, and he came back all right."

"Do you see them often?"

"Almost every day. And little Helen comes every day, you know, for her lessons."

"Is she as pretty as she used to be?"

"Oh yes—prettier, I think. She is a lovely little creature. Having her so much with me is one of my greatest treats. Alex tries to think that she looks a little as I used to. But that is a compliment so great that I dare not appropriate it."

Dr. Carr stooped and kissed Cousin Helen as if he could not help it. "My *dear* child," he said. That was all; but something in the tone made Katy curious.

"Papa," she said, after dinner, "who is Alex that you and Cousin Helen were talking about?"

"Why, Katy? What makes you want to know?"

"I can't exactly tell—only Cousin Helen looked so;— and you kissed her;—and I thought perhaps it was something interesting."

"So it is," said Dr. Carr, drawing her on to his knee. "I've a mind to tell you about it, Katy, because you're old enough to see how beautiful it is, and wise enough, I hope, not to chatter or ask questions. Alex is the name of somebody who, long ago, when Cousin Helen was well and strong, she loved and expected to marry."

"Oh! Why didn't she?" cried Katy.

"She met with a dreadful accident," continued Dr. Carr. "For a long time they thought she would die. Then she grew slowly better, and the doctors told her that she might live a good many years, but that she would have to lie on her sofa always, and be helpless and a cripple."

"Alex felt dreadfully when he heard this. He wanted to marry Cousin Helen just the same, and be her nurse, and take care of her always; but she would not consent. She broke the engagement, and told him that some day she hoped he would love somebody else well enough to marry her. So, after a good many years, he did, and now he and his wife live next door to Cousin Helen,

84

and are her dearest friends. Their little girl is named 'Helen'. All their plans are talked over with her, and there is nobody in the world they think so much of."

"But doesn't it make Cousin Helen feel bad when she sees them walking about and enjoying themselves, and she can't move?" asked Katy.

"No," said Dr. Carr, "it doesn't; because Cousin Helen is half an angel already, and loves other people better than herself. I'm very glad she could come here for once. She's an example to us all, Katy, and I couldn't ask anything better than to have my little girls take pattern after her."

"It must be *awful* to be ill," soliloquized Katy, after Papa was gone. "Why, if I had to stay in bed a whole week—I should *die*, I know I should."

Poor Katy! It seemed to her, as it does to almost all young people, that there is nothing in the world so easy as to die, the moment things go wrong!

This conversation with Papa made Cousin Helen doubly interesting in Katy's eyes. "It was just like something in a book," to be in the same house with the heroine of a love story so sad and sweet.

The play that afternoon was much interrupted, for every few minutes somebody had to run in and see if it wasn't four o'clock. The instant the hour came, all six children galloped upstairs.

"I think we'll tell stories this time," said Cousin Helen.

So they told stories. Cousin Helen's were the best of all. There was one about a robber, which sent delightful chills creeping down all their backs. All but Philly. He was so excited that he grew warlike.

"I ain't afraid of robbers," he declared, strutting up and down. "When they come, I shall just cut them in two with my sword which Papa gave me. They did

85

come once. I did cut them in two—three, five, eleven, of 'em. You'll see!"

But that evening, after the younger children were gone to bed, and Katy and Clover were sitting in the Blue Room, a lamentable howling was heard from the nursery. Clover ran to see what was the matter. Behold—there was Phil, sitting up in bed, and crying for help.

"There's robbers under the bed," he sobbed; "ever so many robbers."

"Why, no, Philly!" said Clover, peeping under the valance to satisfy him; "there isn't anybody there."

"Yes, there is, I tell you," declared Phil, holding her tight. "I heard one. They were *chewing my* overshoes."

"Poor little fellow!" said Cousin Helen, when Clover having pacified Phil, came back to report. "It's a warning against robber stories. But this one ended so well, that I didn't think of anybody's being frightened."

It was no use, after this, for Aunt Izzie to make rules about going into the Blue Room. She might as well have ordered flies to keep away from a sugar-bowl. By hook or by crook, the children *would* get upstairs. Whenever Aunt Izzie went in, she was sure to find them there, just as close to Cousin Helen as they could get. And Cousin Helen begged her not to interfere.

"We have only three or four days to be together," she said. "Let them come as much as they like. It won't hurt me a bit."

Little Elsie clung with a passionate love to this new friend. Cousin Helen had sharp eyes. She saw the wistful look in Elsie's face at one, and took special pains to be sweet and tender to her. This preference made Katy jealous. She couldn't bear to share her cousin with anybody.

When the last evening came, and they went up after

tea to the Blue Room, Cousin Helen was opening a box which had just come by Express. "It is a Goodbye Box," she said. "All of you must sit down in a row, and when I hide my hands behind me, *so*, you must choose in turn which you will take."

So they all chose in turn, "Which hand will you have, the right or the left?" and Cousin Helen, with the air of a wise fairy, brought out from behind her pillow something pretty for each one. First came a vase exactly like her own, which Katy had admired so much. Katy screamed with delight as it was placed in her hands:

"Oh, how lovely! How lovely!" she cried. "I'll keep it as long as I live and breathe."

"If you do, it'll be the first time you ever kept anything for a week without breaking it," remarked Aunt Izzie.

Next came a pretty purple pocket-book for Clover. It was just what she wanted, for she had lost her portemonnaie. Then a sweet little locket on a bit of velvet ribbon, which Cousin Helen tied round Elsie's neck.

"There's a piece of my hair in it," she said. "Why, Elsie, darling, what's the matter? Don't cry so!"

"Oh, you're s-o beautiful and s-o sweet!" sobbed Elsie; "and you're go-o-ing away."

Dorry had a box of dominoes, and John a solitaire board. For Phil there appeared a book—*The History of the Robber Cat*.

"That will remind you of the night when the thieves came and chewed your overshoes," said Cousin Helen, with a mischievous smile. They all laughed, Phil loudest of all.

Nobody was forgotten. There was a notebook for Papa, and a set of ivory tablets for Aunt Izzie. Even Cecy was remembered. Her present was *The Book of*

Golden Deeds, with all sorts of stories about boys and girls who had done brave and good things. She was almost too pleased to speak.

"Oh, thank you, Cousin Helen!" she said at last. Cecy wasn't a cousin, but she and the Carr children were in the habit of sharing their aunts and uncles, and relations generally, as they did their other good things.

Next day came the sad parting. All the little ones stood at the gate, to wave their pocket-handkerchiefs as the carriage drove away. When it was quite out of sight, Katy rushed off to "weep a little weep", all by herself.

"Papa said he wished we were all like Cousin Helen," she thought, as she wiped her eyes, "and I mean to try though I don't suppose if I tried a thousand years I should ever get to be half so good. I'll study, and keep my things in order, and be ever so kind to the little ones. Dear me—if only Aunt Izzie was Cousin Helen, how easy it would be! Never mind—I'll think about her all the time, and I'll begin tomorrow."

CHAPTER EIGHT

TOMORROW

"Tomorrow I will begin," thought Katy, as she dropped asleep that night. How often we all do so! And what a pity it is that when morning comes and tomorrow is today, we so frequently wake up feeling quite differently; careless or impatient, and not a bit inclined to do the fine things we planned overnight.

Sometimes it seems as if there must be wicked little imps in the world, who are kept tied up so long as the sun shines, but who creep into our bedrooms when we are asleep, to tease us and ruffle our tempers. Else, why, when we go to rest good-natured and pleasant, should we wake up so cross? Now, there was Katy. Her last sleepy thought was an intention to be an angel from that time on, and as much like Cousin Helen as she could; and when she opened her eyes she was all out of sorts, and as fractious as a bear! Old Mary said that she got out of bed on the wrong side. I wonder, by the way, if anybody will ever be wise enough to tell us which side that is, so that we may always choose the other? How wonderful it would be if they could!

You know how, if we begin the day in a cross mood, all sorts of unfortunate accidents seem to occur to add to our vexations. The very first thing Katy did this morning was to break her precious vase—the one Cousin Helen had given her.

It was standing on the bureau with a little cluster of blush-roses in it. The bureau had a swing-glass. While Katy was brushing her hair, the glass tipped a little so that she could not see. At a good-humoured moment, this accident wouldn't have troubled her much. But being out of temper to begin with, it made her angry. She gave the glass a violent push. The lower part swung forward, there was a smash, and the first thing Katy knew the blush-roses lay scattered all over the floor, and Cousin Helen's pretty present was ruined.

Katy just sat down on the carpet and cried as hard as if she had been Phil himself. Aunt Izzie heard her lamenting and came in.

"I'm very sorry," she said, picking up the broken glass, "but it's no more than I expected; you're so careless, Katy. Now don't sit there in that foolish way! Get up and dress yourself. You'll be late for breakfast."

"What's the matter?" asked Papa, noticing Katy's red eyes as she took her seat at the table.

"I've broken my vase," said Katy, dolefully.

"It was extremely careless of you to put it in such a dangerous place," said her aunt. "You might have known that the glass would swing and knock it off." Then, seeing a big tear fall in the middle of Katy's plate, she added: "Really, Katy, you're too big to behave like a baby. Why, Dorry would be ashamed to do so. Pray control yourself!"

This snub did not improve Katys temper. She went on with her breakfast in sulky silence.

"What are you all going to do today?" asked Dr. Carr, hoping to give things a more cheerful turn.

"Swing!" cried John and Dorry both together. "Alexander's put us up a splendid one in the woodshed."

"No, you're not," said Aunt Izzie, in a positive tone; "the swing is not to be used till tomorrow. Remember that, children. Not till tomorrow. And not then, unless I give you leave."

This was unwise of Aunt Izzie. She would have done better to have explained further. The truth was, that Alexander, in putting up the swing, had cracked one of the staples which fastened it to the roof. He meant to get a new one in the course of the day, and, meantime, he had cautioned Miss Carr to let no one use the swing, because it really was not safe. If she had told this to the children, all would have been right; but Aunt Izzie's theory was that young people must obey their elders without explanation.

John, and Elsie, and Dorry, all pouted when they heard this order. Elsie recovered her good humour first.

"I don't care," she said, "because I'm going to be very busy; I've got to write a letter to Cousin Helen about somefing." (Elsie never could quite pronounce the *th*.)

"What?" asked Clover.

"Oh, somefing!" answered Elsie, wagging her head mysteriously. "None of the rest of you must know, Cousin Helen said so; it's a secret she and me has got."

"I don't believe Cousin Helen said so at all," said Katy, crossly. "She wouldn't tell secrets to a silly little girl like you."

"Yes, she would too," retorted Elsie, angrily. "She said I was just as good to trust as if I was ever so big. And she said I was her pet. So there, Katy Carr!"

"Stop arguing," said Aunt Izzie. "Katy, your top drawer is all out of order. I never saw anything look so badly. Go upstairs at once and straighten it, before you do anything else. Children, you must keep in the shade this morning. It's too hot for you to be running about in the sun. Elsie, go into the kitchen and tell Debby I want to speak to her."

"Yes," said Elsie, in an important tone. "And afterwards I am coming back to write my letter to Cousin Helen."

Katy went slowly upstairs, dragging one foot after the other. It was a warm, languid day. Her head ached a little, and her eyes smarted and felt heavy from crying so much. Everything seemed dull and hateful. She said to herself, that Aunt Izzie was very unkind to make her work in vacation, and she pulled the top drawer open with a disgusted groan.

It must be confessed that Miss Izzie was right. A bureau drawer could hardly look worse than this one did. It reminded one of the White Knight's recipe for a pudding, which began with blotting-paper, and ended with sealing-wax and gunpowder. All sorts of things were mixed together, as if somebody had put in a long stick, and stirred them up well. There were books and paint-boxes and bits of scribbled paper, and lead pencils and brushes. Stocking legs had come unrolled, and twisted themselves about pocket-handkerchiefs, and ends of ribbon, and linen collars. Rules, all crushed out of shape, stuck up from under the heavier things, and sundry little paper boxes lay empty on top, the treasures they once held having sifted down to the bottom of the drawer, and disappeared beneath the general mass.

It took much time and patience to bring order out of this confusion. But Katy knew that Aunt Izzie would he up by and by, and she dared not stop till all was done. By the time it was finished, she was very tired. Going downstairs, he met Elsie coming up with a slate in her hand, which, as soon as she saw Katy, she put behind her.

"You mustn't look." she said, "it's my letter to Cousin Helen. Nobody but me knows the secret. It's all written, and I'm going to send it to the office. See—there's a stamp on it;" and she exhibited a corner of the slate. Sure enough, there was a stamp stuck on the frame.

"You little goose!" said Katy, impatiently: "you can't send *that* to the post office. Here, give me the slate. I'll copy what you've written on paper, and Papa'll give you an envelope."

"No, no," cried Elsie, struggling, "you mustn't! You'll see what I have said, and Cousin Helen said I wasn't to tell. It's a secret. Let go of my slate. I say! I'll tell Cousin Helen what a mean girl you are, and then she won't love you a bit."

"There, then, take your old slate!" said Katy, giving her a vindictive push. Elsie slipped, screamed caught at the banisters, missed them and, rolling over and over. fell with a thump on the hall floor.

It wasn't much of a fall, only half a dozen steps. but the bump was a hard one, and Elsie roared as if she had been half killed. Aunt Izzie and Mary came rushing to the spot.

"Katy—pushed—me," sobbed Elsie. "She wanted me to tell her my secret, and I wouldn't. She's a bad, naughty girl!"

"Well, Katy Carr, I *should* think you'd be ashamed of yourself," said Aunt Izzie, "wreaking your temper on your poor little sister! I think your Cousin Helen will be surprised when she hears this. There, there, Elsie! Don't cry any more, dear. Come upstairs with me. I'll put on some arnica, and Katy shan't hurt you again."

So they went upstairs. Katy, left below, felt very miserable: repentant, defiant, discontented, and sulky all at once. She knew in her heart that she had not meant to hurt Elsie, and was thoroughly ashamed of that push; but Aunt Izzie's hint about telling Cousin Helen had made her too angry to allow of her confessing this to herself or anybody else.

"I don't care!" she murmured, choking back her tears. "Elsie is a real cry-baby, anyway. And Aunt Izzie always takes her part. Just because I told the little silly not to go and send a great heavy slate to the post office!"

She went out by the side door into the yard. As she passed the shed the new swing caught her eye.

"How exactly like Aunt Izzie," she thought, "ordering the children not to swing till she gives them leave! I suppose she thinks it's too hot, or something. *I* shan't mind her, anyhow."

She seated herself in the swing. It was a first-rate one, with a broad comfortable seat, and thick new ropes. The seat hung just the right distance from the floor. Alexander was a capital hand at putting up swings, and the woodshed the nicest possible spot in which to have one.

It was a big place, with a very high roof. There was not much wood left in it just now, and the little there was, was piled neatly about the sides of the shed, so as to leave plenty of room. The place felt cool and dark, and the motion of the swing seemed to set the breeze blowing. It waved Katy's hair like a great fan, and made her dreamy and quiet. All sorts of sleepy ideas began to flit through her brain. Swinging to and fro like the pendulum of a great clock, she gradually rose higher and higher, driving herself along by the motion of her body, and striking the floor smartly with her foot, at every sweep. Now she was at the top of the high arched door. Then she could almost touch the cross-beam above it, and through the small square window could see pigeons sitting and pluming themselves on the eaves of the barn, and white clouds blowing over the blue sky. She had never swung so high before. It was like flying, she thought, and she bent and curved more strongly in the seat, trying to send herself yet higher, and graze the roof with her toes.

Suddenly, at the very highest point of the sweep, there was a sharp noise of cracking. The swing gave a violent twist, spun half round, and tossed Katy into the air. She clutched the rope—felt it dragged from her grasp—then, down—down—down—she fell. All grew dark, and she knew no more.

When she opened her eyes she was lying on the sofa in the dining-room. Clover was kneeling beside her with a pale, scared face, and Aunt Izzie was dropping something cold and wet on her forehead.

"What's the matter?" asked Katy, faintly.

"Oh, she's alive—she's alive!" and Clover put her arms round Katy's neck and sobbed.

"Hush, dear!" Aunt Izzie's voice sounded unusually gentle. "You've had a bad tumble, Katy. Don't you recollect?"

"A tumble? Oh, yes—out of the swing!" said Katy, as it all came slowly back to her. "Did the rope break, Aunt Izzie? I can't remember about it."

"No, Katy, not the rope. The staple came out of the roof. It was a cracked one, and not safe. Don't you recollect my telling you not to swing today? Did you forget?"

"No, Aunt Izzie—I didn't forget. I—" but here Katy broke down. She closed her eyes, and big tears rolled from under the lids.

"Don't cry," whispered Clover, crying herself, "please don't. Aunt Izzie isn't going to scold you." But Katy was too weak and shaken not to cry.

"I think I'd like to go upstairs and lie on the bed," she said. But when she tried to get off the sofa, everything swam before her, and she fell back again on the pillow.

"Why, I can't stand up!" she gasped, looking very much frightened.

"I'm afraid you've given yourself a sprain somewhere," said Aunt Izzie, who looked rather frightened herself. "You'd better lie still a while, dear, before you try to move. Ah, here's the doctor! Well, I *am* glad." And she went forward to meet him. It wasn't Papa, but Dr. Alsop, who lived quite near them.

"I am so relieved that you could come," Aunt Izzie said. "My brother is gone out of town, not to return till tomorrow, and one of the little girls has had a bad fall."

95

Dr. Alsop sat down beside the sofa and counted Katy's pulse. Then he began feeling all over her.

"Can you move this leg?" he asked.

Katy gave a feeble kick.

"And this?"

The kick was a good deal more feeble.

"Did that hurt you?" asked Dr. Alsop, seeing a look of pain on her face.

"Yes, a little," replied Katy, trying hard not to cry.

"In your back, eh? Was the pain high up or low down?" And the doctor punched Katy's spine for some minutes, making her squirm uneasily.

"I'm afraid she's done some mischief," he said at last, "but it's impossible to tell yet exactly what. It may be only a twist, or a slight sprain," he added, seeing a look of terror on Katy's face. "You'd better get her upstairs and undress her as soon as you can, Miss Carr. I'll leave a prescription to rub her with." And Dr. Alsop took out a bit of paper and began to write.

"Oh, must I go to bed?" said Katy. "How long will I have to stay there, doctor?"

"That depends on how fast you get well," replied the doctor; "not long, I hope. Perhaps only a few days."

"A few days!" repeated Katy, in a despairing tone.

After the doctor was gone, Aunt Izzie and Debby lifted Katy, and carried her slowly upstairs. It was not easy, for every motion hurt her, and the sense of being helpless hurt most of all. She couldn't help crying after she was undressed and put into bed. It all seemed so dreadful and strange. If only Papa was here, she thought. But Dr. Carr had gone into the country to see somebody who was very sick, and couldn't possibly be back till tomorrow.

Such a long, long afternoon that was! Aunt Izzie sent up some dinner, but Katy couldn't eat. Her lips were

96

parched and her head ached violently. The sun began to pour in, the room grew warm. Flies buzzed in the window, and tormented her by lighting on her face. Little prickles of pain ran up and down her back. She lay with her eyes shut, because it hurt to keep them open, and all sorts of uneasy thoughts went rushing through her mind.

"Perhaps, if my back is really sprained, I shall have to lie here as much as a week," she said to herself. "Oh, dear, dear! I *can't*. The vacation is only eight weeks and I was going to do such lovely things! How can people be so patient as Cousin Helen when they have to lie still? Won't she be sorry when she hears! Was it really yesterday that she went away? It seems a year. If only I hadn't got into that nasty old swing!" And then Katy began to imagine how it would have been if she *hadn't*, and how she and Clover had meant to go to Paradise that afternoon. They might have been there under the cool trees now. As these thoughts ran through her mind, her head grew hotter and her position in the bed more uncomfortable.

Suddenly she became conscious that the glaring light from the window was shaded, and that the wind seemed to be blowing freshly over her. She opened her heavy eyes. The blinds were shut, and there beside the bed sat little Elsie, fanning her with a palm-leaf fan.

"Did I wake you up, Katy?" she asked, in a timid voice.

Katy looked at her with startled, amazed eyes.

"Don't be frightened," said Elsie, "I won't disturb you. Johnny and me are *so* sorry you're ill;" and her little lips trembled. "But we mean to keep quiet, and never bang the nursery door, or make noises on the stairs, till you're all well again. And I've brought you somefing real nice. Some of it's from John, and some from me. It's because you got tumbled out of the swing. See!" And Elsie pointed triumphantly to a chair, which she had pulled up close to the bed, and on which were solemnly set forth: 1st, a pewter tea set; 2nd, a box with a glass lid, on which flowers were painted; 3rd, a jointed doll; 4th, a transparent slate; and lastly, two new lead pencils!

"They're all yours—yours to keep," said generous little Elsie. "You can have Pikery too if you want. Only he's pretty big, and I'm afraid he'd be lonely without me. Don't you like the fings, Katy? They're real pretty!"

It seemed to Katy as if the hottest sort of a coal of fire was burning into the top of her head as she looked at the treasures on the chair, and then at Elsie's face all lighted up with affectionate self-sacrifice. She tried to speak, but began to cry instead, which frightened Elsie very much.

"Does it hurt you so bad?" she asked, crying too from sympathy.

"Oh no! It isn't *that*," sobbed Katy; "but I was so cross to you this morning, Elsie, and pushed you. Oh, please forgive me, please do!"

"Why, it's got well!" said Elsie, surprised. "Aunt Izzie put a fing out of a bottle on it, and the bump all went away. Shall I go and ask her to put some on you too—I will." And she ran toward the door.

"Oh no!" cried Katy; "don't go away, Elsie. Come here and kiss me instead."

Elsie turned, as if doubtful whether this invitation could be meant for her. Katy held out her arms. Elsie ran right into them, and the big sister and the little exchanged an embrace which seemed to bring their hearts closer together than they had ever been before.

"You're the most *precious* little darling!" murmured Katy, clasping Elsie tight. "I've been just horrid to you,

Elsie. But I'll never be again. You shall play with me and Clover, and Cecy, just as much as you like, and write notes in all the post offices, and everything else."

"Oh goody, goody!" cried Elsie, executing little skips of transport. "How sweet you are, Katy! I mean to love you next best to Cousin Helen and Papa! And"—racking her brains for some way of repaying this wonderful kindness—"I'll tell you the secret, if you want me to *very* much. I am sure Cousin Helen would let me."

"No," said Katy; "never mind about the secret. I don't want you to tell it to me. Sit down by the bed, and fan me some more instead."

"No!" persisted Elsie, who, now that she had made up her mind to part with the treasured secret, could not bear to be stopped. "Cousin Helen gave me a half-dollar, and told me to give it to Debby, and tell her she was much obliged to her for making her such nice things to eat. And I did. And Debby was very pleased. And I wrote Cousin Helen a letter, and told her that Debby liked the half-dollar. That's the secret! Isn't it a nice one? Only you mustn't tell anybody about it, ever—just as long as you live."

"No!" said Katy, smiling faintly. "I won't."

All the rest of the afternoon Elsie sat beside the bed with her palm-leaf fan, keeping off the flies, and shooing the other children when they peeped in at the door. "Do you really like to have me here?" she asked, more than once, and smiled, oh, *so* triumphantly! when Katy said "Yes!" But though Katy said yes, I am afraid it was only half the truth, for the sight of the dear little forgiving girl, whom she had treated unkindly, gave her more pain than pleasure.

"I'll be *so* good to her when I get well," she thought to herself, tossing uneasily to and fro.

Aunt Izzie slept in her room that night. Katy was feverish. When morning came and Dr. Carr returned, he found her in a good deal of pain, hot and restless, with wide-open, anxious eyes.

"Papa!" she cried the first thing. "Must I lie here as much as a week?"

"My darling, I'm afraid you must," replied her father, who looked worried, and very grave.

"Dear, dear!" sobbed Katy. "How can I bear it?"

CHAPTER NINE

DISMAL DAYS

If anybody had told Katy, that first afternoon, that at the end of a week she would still be in bed, and in pain, and with no time fixed for getting up, I think it would have almost killed her. She was so restless and eager that to lie still seemed one of the hardest things in the world. But to lie still, and have her back ache all the time, was worse yet. Day after day she asked Papa with quivering lips: "May not I get up and go downstairs this morning?" And when he shook his head the lip would quiver more, and tears would come. But if she tried to get up it hurt her so much that in spite of herself she was glad to sink back again on the soft pillows and mattress, which felt so comfortable to her poor bones.

Then there came a time when Katy didn't ever ask to be allowed to get up. A time when sharp, dreadful

100

pain, such as she never imagined before, took hold of her. When days and nights got all confused and tangled up together, and Aunt Izzie never seemed to go to bed. A time when Papa was constantly in her room. When other doctors came and stood over her, and punched and felt her back, and talked to each other in low whispers. It was all like a long, bad dream, from which she couldn't wake up, though she tried ever so hard. Now and then she would rouse a little, and catch the sound of voices, or be aware that Clover or Elsie stood at the door, crying softly; or that Aunt Izzie, in creaking slippers, was going about the room on tiptoe. Then all these things would slip away again, and she would drop off into a dark place where there was nothing but pain, and sleep, which made her forget pain, and so seemed the best thing in the world.

We will hurry over this time, for it is hard to think of our bright Katy in such a sad plight. By and by the pain grew less, and the sleep quieter. Then, as the pain became easier still, Katy woke up as it were—began to take notice of what was going an about her; to put questions.

"How long have I been ill?" she asked one morning.

"It is four weeks yesterday," replied Papa.

"Four weeks!" said Katy. "Why, I didn't know it was so long as that. Was I very ill, Papa?"

"Very, dear. But you are a great deal better now."

"How did I hurt myself when I tumbled out of the swing?" asked Katy, who was in an unusually wakeful mood.

"I don't believe I could make you understand, dear."

"But try, Papa."

"Well, did you know that you had a long bone down your back called a spine?"

101

"I thought that was a disease," said Katy. "Clover said that Cousin Helen had the spine!"

"No, the spine is a bone. It is made up of a row of smaller bones—or knobs—and in the middle of it is a sort of rope of nerves called the spinal cord. Nerves, you know, are the things we feel with. Well, this spinal cord is rolled up for safe keeping in a soft wrapping called membrane. When you fell out of the swing, you struck one of these knobs and bruised the membrane inside, and the nerve inflamed, and gave you a fever in the back. Do you see?"

"A little," said Katy, not quite understanding, but too tired to question further. After she had rested a while she said: "Is the fever well now, Papa? Can I get up again and go downstairs yet?"

"Not yet, I'm afraid," said Dr. Carr, trying to speak cheerfully.

Katy didn't ask any more questions then. Another week passed, and another. The pain was almost gone. It only came back now and then for a few minutes. She could sleep now, and eat, and be raised in bed without feeling giddy. But still the once active limbs hung heavy and lifeless, and she was not able to walk, or even stand alone.

"My legs feel so queer," she said one morning; "they are just like the Prince's legs which were turned to black marble in the *Arabian Nights*. What do you suppose is the reason, Papa? Won't they feel natural soon?"

"Not soon," answered Dr. Carr. Then he said to himself, "Poor child! She had better know the truth." So he went on aloud, "I am afraid, my darling, that you must make up your mind to stay in bed a long time."

"How long?" said Katy, looking frightened; "a month, more?"

"I can't tell exactly how long," answered her father. "The doctors think as I do that the injury to your spine is one which you will outgrow by and by because you are so young and strong. But it may take a good while to do it. It may be that you will have to lie here for months, or it may be more. The only cure for such a hurt is time and patience. It is hard, darling"—for Katy began to sob wildly,—"but you have hope to help you along. Think of poor Cousin Helen, bearing all these years without hope!"

"Oh, Papa!" gasped Katy between her sobs. "Doesn't it seem dreadful, that just getting into the swing for a few minutes should do so much harm? Such a little thing as that!"

"Yes, such a little thing!" repeated Dr. Carr sadly. "And it was only a little thing too, forgetting Aunt Izzie's order about the swing. Just for the want of the small 'horse-shoe nail' of obedience, Katy."

Years afterwards, Katy told somebody that the six longest weeks of her life were those which followed this conversation with Papa. Now that she knew there was no chance of getting well at once, the days dragged dreadfully. Each seemed duller and more dismal than the day before. She lost heart about herself, and took no interest in anything. Aunt Izzie brought her books, but she didn't want to read, or to sew. Nothing amused her. Clover and Cecy would come to sit with her, but hearing them tell about their plays, and the things they had been doing, made her cry so miserably, that Aunt Izzie wouldn't let them come often. They were very sorry for Katy, but the room was so gloomy, and Katy so cross, that they didn't mind much not being allowed to see her. In those days Katy made Aunt Izzie keep the blinds shut tight, and she lay in the dark, thinking how miserable she was, and how wretched all the rest of her life was going to be. Everybody was very kind and patient with her, but she was too selfishly miserable to notice it. Aunt Izzie ran up and down stairs, and was on her feet all day, trying to get something which would please her, but Katy hardly said "Thank you", and never saw how tired Aunt Izzie looked. So long as she was forced to stay in bed, Katy could not be grateful for anything that was done for her.

But doleful as the days were, they were not so bad as the nights, when, after Aunt Izzie was asleep, Katy would lie wide awake, and have long, hopeless fits of crying. At these times she would think of all the plans she had made for doing beautiful things when she was grown up. "And now I shall never do any of them," she would say to herself, "only just lie here. Papa says I may get well by and by, but I shan't, I know I shan't. And even if I do, I shall have wasted all these years, and the others will grow up and get ahead of me, and I shan't be a comfort to them or to anybody else. Oh, dear! Oh, dear! How dreadful it is!"

The first thing which broke in upon this sad state of affairs, was a letter from Cousin Helen, which Papa brought one morning and handed to Aunt Izzie.

"Helen tells me she is going home this week," said Aunt Izzie from the window, where she had gone to read the letter. "Well, I'm sorry, but I think she's quite right not to stop. It's just as she says: one invalid at a time *is* enough in a house. I'm sure I have my hands full with Katy."

"Oh, Aunt Izzie!" cried Katy. "Is Cousin Helen coming this way when she goes home? Oh, do make her stop! If it's just for one day, do ask her! I want to see her so much! I can't tell you how much! Won't you? Please! Please, dear Papa!"

She was almost crying with eagerness.

"Why, yes, darling, if you wish it so much," said Dr. Carr. "It will cost Aunt Izzie some trouble, but she's so kind that I'm sure she'll manage it if it is to give you so much pleasure. Can't you, Izzie?" And he looked eagerly at his sister.

"Of course I will!" said Miss Izzie, heartily. Katy was so glad, that, for the first time in her life, she threw her arms of her own accord round Aunt Izzie's neck and kissed her.

"Thank you, dear Aunty!" she said.

Aunt Izzie looked as pleased as could be. She had a warm heart hidden under her fidgety ways—only Katy had never been ill before, to find it out.

For the next week Katy was feverish with expectation. At last Cousin Helen came. This time Katy was not on the steps to welcome her, but after a little while Papa brought Cousin Helen in his arms, and sat her in a big chair beside the bed.

"How dark it is!" she said, after they had kissed each other and talked for a minute or two. "I can't see your face at all. Would it hurt your eyes to have a little more light?"

"Oh no!" answered Katy. "It doesn't hurt my eyes, only I hate to have the sun come in. It makes me feel worse somehow."

"Push the blinds open a little bit, then, Clover;" and Clover did so.

"Now I can see," said Cousin Helen.

It was certainly a forlorn-looking child which she saw lying before her. Katy's face had grown thin, and her eyes had red circles about them from continual crying. Her hair had been brushed twice that morning by Aunt Izzie, but Katy had run her fingers impatiently through it, till it stood out above her head like a frowzy bush. She wore a calico dressing-gown, which though clean, was particularly ugly in pattern; and the room, for all its tidiness, had a dismal look, with the chairs set up against the wall, and a row of medicine bottles on the chimneypiece.

"I'sn't it horrid?" sighed Katy, as Cousin Helen looked around. "Everything's horrid. But I don't mind so much now that you've come. Oh, Cousin Helen, I've had such a dreadful, *dreadful* time!"

"I know," said her cousin pityingly. "I've heard all about it, Katy. and I'm so very sorry for you. It is a hard trial, my poor darling."

"But how do *you* do it?" cried Katy. "How do you manage to be so sweet and beautiful and patient, when you're feeling badly all the time, and can't do anything, or walk, or stand?"—her voice was lost in sobs.

Cousin Helen didn't say anything for a little while. She just sat and stroked Katy's hand.

"Katy." she said at last, "has Papa told you that he thinks you are going to get well by and by?"

"Yes," replied Katy, "he did say so. But perhaps it won't be for a long, long time. And I wanted to do so many things. And now I can't do anything at all!"

"What sort of things?"

"Study, and help people, and become famous. And I wanted to teach the children. Mamma said I must take care of them. and I meant to. And now I can't go to school or learn anything myself. And if I ever do get well, the children will be almost grown up, and they won't need me."

"But why must you wait till you get well?" asked Cousin Helen, smiling.

"Why, Cousin Helen, what can I do lying here in bed?"

"A good deal. Shall I tell you. Katy, what it seems to me that I should say to myself if I were in your place?"

106

"Yes, please," replied Katy. wonderingly.

"I should say this: 'Now, Katy Carr, you wanted to go to school and learn to be wise and useful, and here's a chance for you. God is going to let you go to *His* school—where He teaches all sorts of beautiful things to people. Perhaps He will only keep you for one term, or perhaps it may be for three or four; but whichever it is, you must make the very most of the chance, because He gives it to you Himself.' "

"But what is the school" asked Katy. "I don't know what you mean."

"It is called The School of Pain," replied Cousin Helen, with her sweetest smile. "And the place where the lessons are to be learned is this room of yours. The rules of the school are pretty hard, but the good scholars, who keep them best, find out after a while how right and kind they are. And the lessons aren't easy, either, but the more you study the more interesting they become."

"What are the lessons?" asked Katy, getting interested, and beginning to feel as if Cousin Helen were telling her a story.

"Well, there's the lesson of Patience. That's one of the hardest studies. You can't learn much of it at a time, but every bit you get by heart makes the next bit easier. And there's the lesson of Cheerfulness. And the lesson of Making the Best of Things."

"Sometimes there isn't anything to make the best of," remarked Katy, dolefully.

"Yes there is, always! Everything in the world has two handles. Didn't you know that? One is a smooth handle. If you take hold of it the thing comes up lightly and easily, but if you seize the rough handle it hurts your hand and the thing is hard to lift. Some people always manage to get hold of the wrong handle."

"Is Aunt Izzie a 'thing'?" asked Katy. Cousin Helen was glad to hear her laugh.

"Yes, Aunt Izzie is a *thing*—and she has a nice pleasant handle too, if you just try to find it. And the children are 'things' also, in one sense. All their handles are different. You know human beings aren't made just alike, like red flower-pots. We have to feel and guess before we can make out just how other people go, and how we ought to take hold of them. It is very interesting, I advise you to try it. And while you are trying, you will learn all sorts of things which will help you to help others."

"If only I could!" sighed Katy. "Are there any other studies in the school, Cousin Helen?"

"Yes, there's the lesson of Hopefulness. That class has ever so many teachers. The Sun is one. He sits outside the window all day waiting a chance to slip in and get at his pupil. He's a first-rate teacher too. I wouldn't shut him out if I were you."

"Every morning when I woke up the first thing, I would say to myself: 'I am going to get well, so Papa thinks. Perhaps it may be tomorrow. So, in case this *should* be the last day of my sickness, let me spend it *beautifully*, and make my sick-room so pleasant that everybody will like to remember it."

"Then, there is one more lesson, Katy—the lesson of Neatness. School-rooms must be kept in order, you know. A sick person ought to be as fresh and dainty as a rose."

"But it is such a fuss," pleaded Katy. "I don't believe you've any idea what a bother it is to be always nice and in order. You never were careless like me, Cousin Helen; you were born neat."

"O, was I?" said her cousin. "Well, Katy, we won't dispute that point: but I'll tell you a story, if you like, about a girl I once knew, who *wasn't* born neat."

"Oh, do! " cried Katy, enchanted. Cousin Helen had done her good already. She looked brighter and less listless than for days.

"This girl was quite young," continued Cousin Helen. "She was strong and active, and liked to run, and climb, and ride, and do all sorts of jolly things. One day something happened—an accident—and they told her that all the rest of her life she had got to lie on her back and suffer pain, and never walk any more, or do any of the things she enjoyed most."

"Just like you and me!" whispered Katy, squeezing Cousin Helen's hand.

"Something like me; but not so much like you, because, you know, we hope *you* are going to get well one of these days. The girl didn't mind it so much when they first told her, for she was so ill that she felt sure she should die. But when she got better, and began to think of the long life which lay before her, that was worse than ever the pain had been. She was so wretched that she didn't care what became of anything, or how anything looked. She had no Aunt Izzie to look after things, so her room soon got into a dreadful state. It was full of dust and confusion, and dirty spoons and phials of physic. She kept the blinds shut, and let her hair tangle any way, and altogether was a dismal spectacle.

"This girl had a dear old father," went on Cousin Helen, "who used to come every day and sit beside her bed. One morning he said to her:

" 'My daughter, I'm afraid you've got to live ill this room for a long time. Now, there's one thing I want you to do for my sake.' "

" 'What is that?' she asked, surprised to hear there was anything left which she could *do* for anybody.

" 'I want you to turn out all these physic bottles, and

make your room pleasant and pretty for *me* to come and sit in. You see, I shall spend a good deal of my time here! Now, I don't like dust and darkness. I like to see flowers on the table, and sunshine in at the window. Will you do this to please me?' "

" 'Yes,' said the girl, but she gave a sigh, and I am afraid she felt as if it was going to be a dreadful trouble.

" 'Then, another thing,' continued her father, 'I want *you* to look pretty. Can't nightgowns and wrappers be trimmed and made becoming just as much as dresses? A sick woman who isn't neat is a disagreeable object. Do, to please me, send for something pretty, and let me see you looking nice again. I can't bear to have my Helen turn into a slattern.' "

"Helen!" exclaimed Katy, with wide-open eyes. "Was it *you*?"

"Yes," said her cousin, smiling. "It was I, though I didn't mean to let the name slip out so soon. So, after my father was gone away, I sent for a looking-glass. Such a sight, Katy! My hair was a perfect mouse's nest, and I had frowned so much that my forehead was all criss-crossed with lines of pain till it looked like an old woman's."

Katy stared at Cousin Helen's smooth brow and glossy hair. "I can't believe it," she said; "your hair never could be rough."

"Yes it was—worse, a great deal, than yours looks now. But that peep in the glass did me good. l began to think how selfishly I was behaving, and to desire to do better. And after that, when the pain came on, I used to lie and keep my forehead smooth with my fingers, and try not to let my face show what I was enduring. So by and by the wrinkles wore away, and though I am a good deal older now, they have never come back."

110

"It was a great deal of trouble at first to have to think and plan to keep my room and myself looking nice. But after a while it grew to be a habit, and then it became easy. And the pleasure it gave my dear father repaid for all. He had been proud of his active, healthy girl, but I think she was never such a comfort to him as his sick one, lying there in her bed. My room was his favourite sitting-place, and he spent so much time there, that now the room, and everything in it, makes me think of him."

There were tears in Cousin Helen's eyes as she ceased speaking. But Katy looked bright and eager. It seemed somehow to be a help, as well as a great surprise, that ever there should have been a time when Cousin Helen was less perfect than she was now.

"Do you really think I could do so too?" she asked.

"Do what? Comb your hair!" Cousin Helen was smiling now.

"Oh no! Be nice and sweet and patient, and a comfort to people. You know what I mean."

"I am sure you can if you try."

"But what would you do first?" asked Katy, who, now that her mind had grasped a new idea, was eager to begin.

"Well, first I would open the blinds, and make the room look a little less dismal. Are you taking all those medicines in the bottles now?"

"No, only that big one with the blue label."

"Then you might ask Aunt Izzie to take away the others. And I'd get Clover to pick a bunch of fresh flowers every day for your table. By the way, I don't see the little white vase."

"No, it got broken the very day after you went away: the day I fell out of the swing," said Katy sorrowfully.

"Never mind, pet; don't look so doleful. I know the

111

tree those vases grow upon, and you shall have another. Then, after the room is made pleasant, I would have all my lesson-books fetched up if I were you, and I would study a couple of hours every morning."

"Oh!" cried Katy, making a wry face at the idea.

Cousin Helen smiled. "I know," said she, "it sounds like dull work, learning geography and doing sums up here all by yourself. But I think if you make the effort you'll be glad by and by. You won't lose so much ground, you see—won't slip back quite so far in your education. And then, studying will be like working at a garden where things don't grow easily. Every flower you raise will be a sort of triumph, and you will value it twice as much as a common flower which has cost no trouble."

"Well," said Katy, rather forlornly, "I'll try. But it won't be a bit nice studying without anybody to study with one. Is there anything else, Cousin Helen?"

Just then the door creaked, and Elsie timidly put her head into the room.

"Oh, Elsie, run away!" cried Katy. "Cousin Helen and I are talking. Don't come just now."

Katy didn't speak unkindly, but Elsie's face fell, and she looked disappointed. She said nothing, however, but shut the door and stole away.

Cousin Helen watched this little scene without speaking. For a few minutes after Elsie was gone, she seemed to be thinking.

"Katy", she said at last, "you were saying just now that one of the things you were sorry about was that while you were ill you could be of no use to the children. Do you know, I don't think you have any reason for being sorry."

"Why not?" said Katy, astonished.

"Because you *can* be of use. It seems to me that you

112

have more of a chance with the children now, than you ever could have had when you were well, and flying about as you used to. You might do almost anything you liked with them."

"I can't think what you mean," said Katy, sadly. "Why, Cousin Helen, half the time I don't even know where they are, or what they are doing. And I can't get up and go after them, you know."

"But you can make your room such a delightful place that they will want to come to you! Don't you see, a sick person has one splendid chance—she is always on hand. Everybody who wants her knows just where to go. If people love her, she gets naturally to be the heart of the house. Once make the little ones feel that your room is the place of all others to come to when they are tired, or happy, or grieved, or sorry about anything, and that the Katy who lives there is sure to give them a loving reception—and the battle is won. For you know we never do people good by lecturing; only by living their lives with them, and helping a little here and a little there, to make them better. And when one's own life is laid aside for a while, as yours is now, that is the very time to take up other people's lives, as we can't do when we are scurrying and bustling over our own affairs. But I didn't mean to preach a sermon. I'm afraid you're tired."

"No, I'm not a bit," said Katy, holding Cousin Helen's hand tight in hers. "You can't think how much better I feel. O, Cousin Helen, I *will* try!"

"It won't be easy," replied her cousin. "There will be days when your head aches, and you feel cross and fretted, and don't want to think of anyone but yourself. And there'll be other days when Clover and the rest will come in, as Elsie did just now, and you will be

113

doing something else, and will feel as if their coming was a bother. But you must recollect that every time you forget, and are impatient or selfish, you chill them and drive them further away. They are loving little things, and are so sorry for you now, that nothing you do makes them angry. But by and by they will get used to having you sick, and if you haven't won them as friends they will grow away from you as they get older." Just then Dr. Carr came in.

"Oh, Papa! you haven't come to take Cousin Helen, have you?" cried Katy.

"Indeed I have," said her father. "I think the big invalid and the little invalid have talked quite long enough. Cousin Helen looks tired." For a minute Katy felt just like crying. But she choked back the tears. "My first lesson in patience," she said to herself, and managed to give a faint, watery smile as Papa looked at her.

"That's right, dear," whispered Cousin Helen, as she bent forward to kiss her. "And one last word, Katy. In this school to which you and I belong, there is one great comfort, and that is that the Teacher is always at hand. He never goes away. If things puzzle us, there He is, close by, ready to explain and make all easy. Try to think of this, darling, and don't be afraid to ask Him for help if the lesson seems too hard."

Katy had a strange dream that night. She thought she was trying to study a lesson out of a book which wouldn't come quite open. She could just see a little bit of what was inside, but it was in a language which she did not understand. She tried in vain: not a word could she read; and yet, for all that, it looked so interesting that she longed to go on.

"Oh, if somebody would only help me!" she cried impatiently.

Suddenly a hand came over her shoulder and took hold of the book. It opened at once, and showed the whole page. And then the forefinger of the hand began to point to line after line, and as it moved the words became plain, and Katy could read them easily. She looked up. There, stooping over her, was a great beautiful Face. The eyes met hers. The lips smiled.

"Why didn't you ask me before, little scholar?" said a voice.

"Why, it is *You*—just as Cousin Helen told me!" cried Katy.

She must have spoken in her sleep, for Aunt Izzie half woke up, and said:

"What is it? Do you want anything?"

The dream broke, and Katy roused, to find herself in bed, with the first sunbeams struggling in at the window, and Aunt Izzie raised on her elbow, looking at her with a sort of sleepy wonder.

CHAPTER TEN

ST. NICHOLAS AND ST. VALENTINE

"What are the children all doing today?" said Katy, laying down *Norway and the Norwegians*, which she was reading for the fourth time. "I haven't seen them since breakfast."

Aunt Izzie, who was sewing on the other side of the room, looked up from her work.

"I don't know," she said; "they're over at Cecy's, or somewhere. They'll be back before long, I guess."

Her voice sounded a little odd and mysterious, but Katy didn't notice it.

"I thought of such a nice plan yesterday," she went on. "That was that all of them should hang their stockings up here tomorrow night instead of in the nursery. Then I could see them open their presents, you know. Mayn't they, Aunt Izzie? It would be great fun."

"I don't think there will be any objection, replied her aunt. She looked as if she were trying not to laugh. Katy wondered what *was* the matter with her.

It was more than two months now since Cousin Helen went away, and winter had fairly come. Snow was falling outdoors. Katy could see the thick flakes go whirling past the window, but the sight did not chill her. It only made the room look warmer and more cosy. It was a pleasant room now. There was a bright fire in the grate. Everything was neat and orderly, the air was sweet with mignonette, from a little glass of flowers which stood on the table, and the Katy who lay in bed was a very different-looking Katy from the forlorn girl of the last chapter.

Cousin Helen's visit, though it lasted only one day, did great good. Not that Katy grew perfect all at once. None of us do that, even in books. But it is everything to be started in the right path. Katy's feet were on it now; and though she often stumbled and slipped, and often sat down discouraged, she kept on pretty steadily, in spite of bad days, which made her say to herself that she was not getting forward at all.

These bad days, when everything seemed hard, and she herself was cross and fretful, and drove the children out of her room, cost Katy many bitter tears. But after them she would pick herself up, and try

116

again, and harder. And I think that in spite of drawbacks, the little scholar, on the whole, was learning her lesson pretty well.

Cousin Helen was a great comfort all this time. She never forgot Katy. Nearly every week some little thing came from her. Sometimes it was a pencil note, written from her sofa. Sometimes it was an interesting book, or a new magazine, or some pretty thing for the room. The crimson wrapper which Katy wore was one of her presents, so were the bright chromes of autumn leaves which hung on the wall, the little stand for the books—all sorts of things. Katy loved to look about her as she lay. All the room seemed full of Cousin Helen and her kindness.

"I wish I had something pretty to put into everybody's stocking," she went on, wistfully; "but I've only got the muffatees for Papa, and these reins for Phil." She took them from under her pillow as she spoke—gay worsted affairs, with bells sewn on here and there. She had knitted them herself, a very little bit at a time.

"There's my pink sash," she said suddenly; "I might give that to Clover. I only wore it once, you know, and I don't *think* I got any spots on it. Would you please fetch it and let me see, Aunt Izzie? It's in the top drawer."

Aunt Izzie brought the sash. It proved to be quite fresh, and they both decided that it would do nicely for Clover.

"You know I shan't want sashes for ever so long," said Katy, in rather a sad tone. "And this is a beauty."

When she spoke next her voice was bright again.

"I wish I had something very nice for Elsie. Do you know, Aunt Izzie—I think Elsie is the dearest little girl that eve was."

"I'm glad you've found it out," said Aunt Izzie, who had always been specially fond of Elsie.

"What she wants most of all is a writing-desk," continued Katy. "And Johnny wants a sled. But, oh dear! those are such big things. And I've only got two dollars and a quarter."

Aunt Izzie marched out of the room without saying anything. When she came back she had something folded up in her hand.

"I didn't know what to give you for Christmas, Katy," she said, "because Helen sends you such a lot of things that there does not seem to be anything you haven't already. So I thought I'd give you this, and let you choose for yourself. But if you've set your heart on getting presents for the children, perhaps you'd rather have it now." So saying, Aunt Izzie laid on the bed a crisp new five-dollar note!

"How good you are!" cried Katy, flushed with pleasure. And indeed Aunt Izzie *did* seem to have grown wonderfully good of late. Perhaps Katy had got hold of her smooth handle!

Being now in possession of seven dollars and a quarter, Katy could afford to be gorgeously generous. She gave Aunt Izzie an exact description of the desk she wanted.

"It's no matter about its being very big," said Katy, "but it must have a blue velvet lining, and an ink-stand with a silver top. And please buy some little sheets of paper and envelopes, and a pen-handle; the prettiest you can find. Oh! and there must be a lock and key. Don't forget that, Aunt Izzie."

"No, I won't. What else?"

"I'd like the sled to be green," went on Katy, "and to have a nice name. 'Sky-Scraper' would be nice, if there was one. Johnny saw a sled once called 'Sky-Scraper', and she said it was splendid. And if there's money enough left, Aunty, won't you buy me a nice book for

Dorry, and another for Cecy, and a silver thimble for Mary? Her old one is full of holes. Oh! and some candy. And something for Debby and Bridget—some little thing, you know. I think that's all!"

Was ever seven dollars and a quarter expected to do so much? Aunt Izzie must have been a witch, indeed, to make it hold out. But she did, and next day all the precious bundles came home. How Katy enjoyed untying the strings!

Everything was exactly right.

"There wasn't any 'Sky-Scraper'," said Aunt Izzie, "so I got 'Snow-Skimmer' instead."

"It's beautiful, and I like it just as well," said Katy, contentedly. "Oh, hide them, hide them!" she cried with sudden terror; "somebody's coming!" But the somebody was only Papa, who put his head into the room as Aunt Izzie, laden with bundles, scuttled across the hall.

Katy was glad to catch him alone. She had a little private secret to talk over with him. It was about Aunt Izzie, for whom she, as yet, had no present.

"I thought perhaps you'd get me a book like that one of Cousin Helen's, which Aunt Izzie liked so much," she said. "I don't recollect the name exactly. It was something about a Shadow. But I've spent all my money."

"Never mind about that," said Dr. Carr. "We'll make that right. *The Shadow of the Cross*—was that it? I'll buy it this afternoon."

"Oh, thank you, Papa! And please get a brown cover, if you can, because Cousin Helen's was brown. And you won't let Aunt Izzie know, will you! Be careful, Papa."

"I'll swallow the book first, brown cover and all," said Papa, making a funny face. He was pleased to see Katy so interested about anything again.

These delightful secrets took up so much of her thoughts, that Katy scarcely found time to wonder at the absence of the children, who generally haunted her room, but who for three days back had hardly been seen. However, after supper they all came up in a body, looking very merry, and as if they had been having a good time somewhere.

"You don't know what we've been doing," began Philly.

"Hush, Phil!" said Clover, in a warning voice. Then she divided the stockings which she held in her hand. And everybody proceeded to hang them up.

Dorry hung his on one side of the fireplace, and John hers exactly opposite. Clover and Phil suspended theirs side by side, on two handles of the bureau.

"I'm going to put mine here, close to Katy, so that she can see it first fing in the morning," said Elsie, pinning hers to the bed-post.

Then they all sat down round the fire to write their wishes on bits of paper, and see whether they would burn, or fly up the chimney. If they did the latter, it was a sign that Santa Claus had them safe, and would bring the things wished for.

John wished for a sled and a doll's tea set, and the continuation of the *Swiss Family Robinson*. Dorry's list ran thus:

> A plum-cake,
> A new Bibel,
> *Harry and Lucy*,
> A Kellidescope,
> Everything else Santa Claus likes.

When they had written these lists they threw them into the fire. The fire gave a flicker just then, and the papers vanished. Nobody saw exactly how. John thought they flew up the chimney, but Dorry said they didn't.

Phil dropped his piece in very solemnly. It flamed for a minute, then sank into ashes.

"There, you won't get it, whatever it was!" said Dorry. "What did you write, Phil?"

"Nofing," said Phil; "only just Philly Carr."

The children shouted.

"I wrote 'a writing-desk' on mine," remarked Elsie, sorrowfully, "but it all burned up."

Katy chuckled when she heard this.

And now Clover produced her list. She read aloud:

> *Serve and Thrive*,
> A pair of kid gloves,
> A muff,
> A good temper!

Then she dropped it into the fire. Behold, it flew straight up the chimney.

"How queer!" said Katy. "None of the rest of them did that."

The truth was that Clover, who was a queer little mortal, had slipped across the room and opened the door just before putting her wishes in. This, of course, made a draught and sent the paper right upwards.

Pretty soon Aunt Izzie came in and swept them all off to bed.

"I know how it will be in the morning," she said, "you'll all be up and racing about as soon as it is light. So you must get your sleep now, if ever."

After they had gone, Katy recollected that nobody had offered to hang a stocking up for her. She felt a little hurt when she thought of it. "But I suppose they forgot," she said to herself.

121

A little later Papa and Aunt Izzie came in, and they filled the stockings. It was great fun. Each was brought to Katy, as she lay in bed, that she might arrange it as she liked.

The toes were stuffed with candy and oranges. Then came the parcels, all shapes and sizes, tied in white paper, with ribbons, and labelled.

"What's that?" asked Dr. Carr, as Aunt Izzie rammed a long, narrow package into Clover's stocking.

"A nail-brush," answered Aunt Izzie; "Clover needed a new one." How Papa and Katy laughed! "I don't believe Santa Claus ever had such a thing before," said Dr. Carr.

"He's a very dirty old gentleman then," observed Aunt Izzie grimly.

The desk and sled were too big to go into any stocking, so they were wrapped in paper and hung beneath the other things. It was ten o'clock before all was done, and Papa and Aunt Izzie went away. Katy lay a long time watching the queer shapes of the stocking legs as they dangled in the firelight. Then she fell asleep.

It seemed only a minute, before something touched her and woke her up. Behold, it was day time, and there was Philly in his nightgown, climbing up on the bed to kiss her! The rest of the children, half dressed, were dancing about with their stockings in their hands.

"Merry Christmas! Merry Christmas!" they cried. "Oh, Katy, such beautiful, *beautiful* things!"

"Oh!" shrieked Elsie, who at that moment spied her desk, "Santa Claus *did* bring it, after all! Why, it's got 'from Katy' written on it! Oh, Katy, it's so sweet, and I'm *so* happy!" and Elsie hugged Katy, and sobbed for pleasure.

But what was that strange thing beside the bed? Katy

stared, and rubbed her eyes. It certainly had not been there when she went so sleep. How had it come?

It was a little evergreen tree planted in a red flower-pot. The pot had stripes of gilt paper stuck on it, and gilt stars and crosses, which made it look very gay. The boughs of the tree were hung with oranges, and nuts, and shiny red apples, and popcorn balls, and strings of bright berries. There were also a number of little packages tied with blue and crimson ribbon, and altogether the tree looked so pretty, that Katy gave a cry of delighted surprise.

"It's a Christmas tree for you, because you're ill, you know!" said the children, all trying to hug her at once.

"We made it ourselves," said Dorry, hopping about on one foot; "I pasted the black stars on the pot."

"And I popped the corn!" cried Philly.

"Do you like it?" asked Elsie, cuddling close to Katy. "That's my present—that one tied with a green ribbon. I wish it was nicer! Don't you want to open them at once!"

Of course Katy wanted to. All sorts of things came out of the little bundles. The children had arranged every parcel themselves. No grown person had been allowed to help in the least.

Elsie's present was a pen-wiper, with a grey flannel kitten on it. Johnnie's, a doll's tea-tray of scarlet tin.

"Isn't it beau-ti-ful?" she said, admiringly.

Dorry's gift, I regret to say, was a huge red-and-yellow spider, which whirred wildly when waved at the end of its string.

"They didn't want me to buy it," he said, "but I did! I thought it would amuse you. Does it amuse you, Katy?"

"Yes indeed," said Katy, laughing and blinking as Dorry waved the spider to and fro before her eyes.

"You can play with it when we are not here and you're all alone, you know," remarked Dorry, highly gratified.

"But you don't notice what the tree's standing upon," said Clover.

It was a chair, a very large and curious one, with a long-cushioned back, which ended in a footstool.

"That's Papa's present," said Clover. "See, it tips back so as to be just like a bed. And Papa said he thinks pretty soon you can lie on it, in the window, where you can see us play."

"Does he really?" said Katy, doubtfully. It still hurt her very much to be touched or moved.

"And see what's tied to the arm of the chair," said Elsie.

It was a little silver bell, with "Katy" engraved on the handle.

"Cousin Helen sent it. It's for you to ring when you want anybody to come," explained Elsie.

More surprises. To the other arm of the chair was fastened a beautiful book. It was of *The Wide, Wide World*—and there was Katy's name written on it, "from her affectionate Cecy". On it stood a great parcel of dried cherries from Mrs. Hall. Mrs. Hall had the most *delicious* dried cherries, the children thought.

"How perfectly lovely everybody is!" said Katy, with grateful tears in her eyes.

That was a pleasant Christmas. The children declared it to be the nicest they had ever had. And though Katy couldn't quite say that, she enjoyed it too, and was very happy.

It was several weeks before she was able to use the chair, but when once she became accustomed to it, it proved very comfortable. Aunt Izzie would dress her in the morning, tip the chair back till it was on a level with the bed, and then, very gently and gradually, draw her over on to it. Wheeling across the room was always painful, but sitting in the window and looking out at the clouds, the people going by, and the children playing in the snow, was delightful. How delightful nobody knows, excepting those who, like Katy, have lain for six months in bed, without a peep at the outside world. Every day she grew brighter and more cheerful.

"How jolly Santa Claus was this year!" she happened to say one day, when she was talking with Cecy. "I wish another saint would come and pay us a visit. But I don't know any more, except Cousin Helen, and she can't."

"There's St. Valentine," suggested Cecy.

"Sure enough. What a bright thought!" cried Katy, clapping her hands. "Oh, Cecy, let's do something funny on Valentine's day! Such a good idea has just popped into my mind."

So the two girls put their heads together and held a long, mysterious confabulation. What it was about we shall see later on.

Valentine's day was the next Friday. When the children came home from school on Thursday afternoon Aunt Izzie met them, and, to their great surprise, told them that Cecy had come to drink tea, and they must all go upstairs and be made nice.

"But Cecy comes most every day," remarked Dorry, who didn't see the connection between this fact and having his face washed.

"Yes; but tonight you are to take tea in Katy's room," said Aunt Izzie. "Here are the invitations—one for each of you."

Sure enough, there was a neat little note for each,

requesting the pleasure of their company at "Queen Katherine's Palace", that afternoon, at six o'clock.

This put quite a different aspect on the affair. The children scampered upstairs, and pretty soon, all nicely brushed and washed, they were knocking formally at the door of the "Palace". How fine it sounded!

The room looked bright and inviting. Katy, in her chair, sat close to the fire, Cecy beside her, and there was a round table all set out with a white cloth and mugs of milk and biscuit, and strawberry jam and doughnuts. In the middle was a loaf of frosted cake. There was something on the icing which looked like pink letters, and Clover, leaning forward, read aloud, "St. Valentine".

"What's that for?" asked Dorry.

"Why, you know this is St. Valentine's Eve," replied Katy. "Debby remembered it, I suppose, so she put that on."

Nothing more was said about St. Valentine just then. But when the last pink letter of his name had been eaten, and the supper had been cleared away, suddenly, as the children sat by the fire, there was a loud rap at the door.

"Who can that be?" said Katy; "please see, Clover!"

So Clover opened the door. There stood Bridget, trying very hard not to laugh, and holding a letter in her hand.

"It's a note as has come for you, Miss Clover," she said.

"For *me*!" cried Clover, much amazed. Then she shut the door, and brought the note to the table.

"How very funny!" she exclaimed, as she looked at the envelope, which was a green-and-white one. There was something hard inside. Clover broke the seal. Out tumbled a small green velvet pin-cushion made in the shape of a clover leaf, with a tiny stem of wire wound with green silk. Pinned to the cushion was a paper with these verses:

> "Some people love roses well,
>   Tulips, gaily dressed,
> Some love violets blue and sweet,—
>   I love Clover best.
>
> "Though she has a modest air,
>   Though no grace she boast,
> Though no gardener call her fair,
>   I love Clover most.
>
> "Butterfly may pass her by,
>   He is but a rover,
> I'm a faithful, loving Bee—
>   And I stick to Clover."

This was the first valentine Clover had ever had. She was perfectly enchanted.

"Oh, who *do* you suppose sent it?" she cried.

But before anybody could answer, there came another loud knock at the door, which made them all jump. Behold, Bridget again, with a second letter!

"It's for you, Miss Elsie, this time," she said with a grin.

There was an instant rush from all the children, and the envelope was torn open in the twinkling of an eye. Inside was a little ivory seal with "Elsie" on it in old English letters, and these rhymes:

> "I know a little girl,
>   She is very dear to me,
> She is just as sweet as honey
>   When she chooses so to be,
> And her name begins with E, and ends with E.

127

"She has brown hair which curls,
    And black eyes for to see
With, teeth like tiny pearls,
    And dimples, one, two—three,
And her name begins with E, and ends with E.

"Her little feet run faster
    Than other feet can flee,
As she brushes quickly past, her
    Voice hums like a bee,
And her name begins with E, and ends with E.

"Do you ask me why I love her?
    Then I shall answer thee,
Because I can't help loving,
    She is so sweet to me,
This little girl whose name begins and ends with 'E'."

"It's just like a fairy story," said Elsie, whose eyes had grown as big as saucers from surprise, while these verses were being read aloud by Cecy.

Another knock! This time there was a perfect handful of letters. Everybody had one. Katy, to her great surprise, had *two*.

"Why, what *can* this be?" she asked. But when she peeped into the second one, she saw Cousin Helen's hand-writing, and she put it into her pocket, till the valentines should be read.

Dorry's was opened first. It had the picture of a pie at the top—I ought to explain that Dorry had lately been having a bad time with the dentist.

"Little Jack Horner
Sat in his corner,
    Eating his Christmas pie,
When a sudden grimace
Spread over his face,

128

And he began loudly to cry.
"His tender Mamma
Heard the sound from afar,
    And hastened to comfort her child;
" 'What aileth my John?'
She inquired in a tone
    Which belied her question mild.
'Oh, Mother,' he said,
'Every tooth in my head
    Jumps and aches and is loose, O my!
And its hurts me to eat
Anything that is sweet—
    So what *will* become of my pie?'"
"It were vain to describe
How he roared and he cried,
    And howled like a miniature tempest;
Suffice it to say
That the very next day
    He had all his teeth pulled by a dentist!"

This valentine made the children laugh for a long time. Johnnie's envelope held a paper doll named "Red Riding Hood." These were the verses:

"I send you my picture, dear Johnnie, to show
    That I'm just as alive as you,
And that you needn't cry over my fate
    Any more, as you used to do.
"The wolf didn't hurt me at all that day,
    For I kicked and fought and cried,
Till he dropped me out of his mouth, and ran
    Away in the woods to hide.
"And Grandma and I·have lived ever since
    In the little brown house so small,
And churned fresh butter and made cream cheeses,
    Nor seen the wolf at all.
"So cry no more for fear I am eaten,

129

The naughty wolf is shot,
And if you will come to tea some evening
You shall see for yourself I'm not."

Johnnie was immensely pleased at this, for Red
Riding Hood was a great favourite of hers.

Philly had a bit of indiarubber in his letter, which
was written with very black ink on a big sheet of
foolscap:

"I was once a naughty man,
And I hid beneath the bed,
To steal your india rubbers,
But I chewed them up instead.
"Then you called out 'Who is there?'
I was thrown most in a fit,
And I let the indiarubbers fall—
All but this little bit.
"I'm sorry for my naughty ways,
And now, to make amends,
I send the chewed piece back again,
And beg we may be friends.
"ROBBER."

"Just listen to mine," said Cecy, who had all along
pretended to be as much surprised as anybody, and
now behaved as if she could hardly wait till Philly's
was finished. Then she read aloud:

"TO CECY
"If I were a bird
And you were a bird,
What would we do?
Why, you should be little and I would be big,
And, side by side on a cherry-tree twig,
We'd kiss with our yellow bills, and coo—
That's what we'd do!

"If I were a fish
And you were a fish,
    What would we do?
We'd frolic, and whisk our little tails,
And play all sorts of tricks with the whales,
And call on the oysters, and order a 'stew',
    That's what we'd do!
"If I were a bee
And you were a bee,
    What would we do?
We'd find a home in a breezy wood,
And store it with honey sweet and good.
You should feed me and I would feed you,
    That's what we'd do!
                                    "VALENTINE."

"I think that's the prettiest of all," said Clover.

"I don't, said Elsie. "I think mine is the prettiest.
Cecy didn't have any seal in hers, either." And she
fondled the little seal, which all this time she had held
in her hand.

"Katy, you ought to have read yours first, because
you are the oldest," said Clover.

"Mine isn't much," replied Katy! and she read:

        "The rose is red, the violet blue,
        Sugar is sweet, and so are you."

"What a mean valentine!" cried Elsie, with flashing
eyes. "It's a great shame, Katy! You ought to have had
the best of all."

Katy could hardly keep from laughing. The fact was
that the verses for the others had taken so long that no
time had been left for writing a valentine to herself.
So, thinking it would excite suspicion to have none,
she had scribbled this old rhyme at the last moment.

131

"It isn't very nice," she said, trying to look as pensive as she could, "but never mind."

"It's a shame!" repeated Elsie, petting her very hard to make up for the injustice.

"Hasn't it been a funny evening" said John; and Dorry replied, "Yes; we never had such good times before Katy was ill, did we?"

Katy heard this with a mingled feeling of pleasure and pain. "I think the children do love me a little more of late," she said to herself. "But, oh! why couldn't have been good to them when I was well and strong!"

She didn't open Cousin Helen's letter until the rest were all gone to bed. I think somebody must have written and told about the valentine party, for instead of a note there were these verses in Cousin Helen's own clear, pretty hand. It wasn't a valentine, because it was too solemn, as Katy explained to Clover next day. "But," she added, "it is a great deal more beautiful than any valentine that ever was written." And Clover thought so too.

These were the verses:

IN SCHOOL

I used to go to a bright school
   Where Youth and Frolic taught in turn;
But idle scholar that I was,
   I liked to play, I would not learn;
So the Great Teacher did ordain
That I should try the School of Pain.

One of the infant class I am
   With little, easy lessons, set
In a great book; the higher class
   Have harder ones than I, and yet
I find mine hard, and can't restrain
My tears while studying thus with Pain.

132

There are two Teachers in the school,
    One has a gentle voice and low,
And smiles upon her scholars, as
    She softly passes to and fro.
Her name is Love; 'tis very plain
She shuns the sharper teacher, Pain.

Or so I sometimes think; and then,
    At other times, they meet and kiss,
And look so strangely like, that I
    Am puzzled to tell how it is,
Or whence the change which makes it vain
To guess if it be—Love or Pain.

They tell me if I study well,
    And learn my lessons,I shall be
Moved upward to that higher class
    Where dear Love teaches constantly;
And I work hard, in hopes to gain
Reward, and get away from Pain.

Yet Pain is sometimes kind, and helps
    Me on when I am very dull;
I thank him often in my heart;
    But Love is far more beautiful;
Under her tender, gentle reign
I must learn faster than of Pain.

So I will do my very best,
    Nor chide the clock. nor call it slow;
That when the Teacher calls me up
    To see if I am fit to go,
I may to Love's high class attain,
And bid a sweet goodbye to Pain.

133

CHAPTER ELEVEN

A NEW LESSON TO LEARN

It was a long time before the children ceased to talk and laugh over that jolly evening. Dorry declared he wished there could be a Valentine's day every week.

"Don't you think St. Valentine would be tired of writing verses?" asked Katy. But she, too, had enjoyed the frolic, and the bright recollection helped her along through the rest of the long, cold winter.

Spring arrived late that year, but the summer, when it came, was a warm one. Katy felt the heat very much. She could not change her seat and follow the breeze about from window to window as other people could. The long burning days left her weak and parched. She hung her head, and seemed to wilt like the flowers in the garden beds. Indeed she was worse off than they, for every evening Alexander gave them a watering with the hose, while nobody was able to bring a watering-pot and pour out what she needed—a shower of cold fresh air.

It wasn't easy to be good-humoured under these circumstances, and one could hardly have blamed Katy if she had sometimes forgotten her resolutions and been cross and fretful. But she didn't—not very often. Now and then bad days came, when she was discouraged and forlorn. But Katy's long year of schooling had taught her self-control, and, as a general thing, her discomforts were borne patiently. She could not help growing pale and thin, however, and Papa saw with concern that as the summer went on, she became too languid to read, or study, or sew, and just sat hour after hour, with folded hands, gazing wistfully out of the window.

He tried the experiment of taking her to drive. But the motion of the carriage, and the being lifted in and out, brought on so much pain, that Katy begged that he would not ask her to go again. So there was nothing to be done but wait for cooler weather. The summer dragged on, and all who loved Katy rejoiced when it was over.

When September came, with cool mornings and nights, and fresh breezes, smelling of pine woods and hill tops, all things seemed to revive, and Katy with them. She began to crochet and to read. After a while she collected her books again, and tried to study as Cousin Helen had advised. But so many idle weeks made it seem harder work than ever. One day she asked Papa to let her take French lessons.

"You see, I'm forgetting all I knew," she said, "and Clover is going to begin this term, and I don't like that she should get so far ahead of me. Don't you think Mr. Berger would be willing to come here, Papa? He does go to houses sometimes."

"I think he would if we asked him," said Dr. Carr, pleased to see Katy waking up with something like life again.

So the arrangement was made. Mr. Berger came twice every week, and sat beside the big chair, correcting Katy's exercises and practising her in the verbs and pronunciation. He was a lively little old Frenchman, and knew how to make lesson time pleasant.

"You take more pains than you used to, Mademoiselle," he said one day; "if you go on so, you shall be my best scholar. And if to hurt the back make you study, it would be well that some other of my young ladies shall do the same."

Katy laughed. But in spite of Mr. Berger and his lessons, and in spite of her endeavours to keep cheerful and busy, this second winter was harder than the first. It is often so with sick people.

There is a sort of excitement in being ill which helps along just at the beginning. But as months go on, and everything grows an old story, and one day follows another, all just alike, and all tiresome, courage is apt to flag and spirits to grow dull. Spring seemed a long, long way off whenever Katy thought about it.

"I wish something would happen," she often said to herself. And something was about to happen. But she little guessed what it was going to be.

"Katy," said Clover, coming in one day in November, "do you know where the camphor is? Aunt Izzie has got *such* a headache."

"No," replied Katy, "I don't. Or—wait—Clover, it seems to me that Debby came for it the other day. Perhaps if you look in her room you'll find it."

"How very queer!" she soliloquized, when Clover was gone; "I never knew Aunt Izzie to have a headache before."

"How is Aunt Izzie?" she asked, when Papa came in at noon.

"Well, I don't know. She has some fever and a bad pain in her head. I have told her that she had better lie still, and not try to get up this evening. Old Mary will come in to undress you, Katy. You won't mind, will you, dear?"

"N-o!" said Katy, reluctantly. But she did mind. Aunt Izzie had grown used to her and her ways. Nobody else suited her so well.

"It seems so strange to have to explain just how every little thing is to be done," she remarked to Clover, rather petulantly. It seemed stranger yet, when

136

the next day, and the next, and the next after that passed, and still no Aunt Izzie came near her. Blessings brighten as they take their flight. Katy began to appreciate for the first time how much she had learned to rely on her aunt. She missed her dreadfully.

"When *is* Aunt Izzie going to get well?" she asked her father. "I want her so much."

"We all want her," said Dr. Carr, who looked disturbed and anxious.

"Is she very ill?" asked Katy, struck by the expression of his face.

"Pretty ill, I'm afraid," he replied. "I'm going to get a regular nurse to take care of her."

Aunt Izzie's attack proved to be typhoid fever. The doctors said that the house must be kept quiet, so John and Dorry and Phil were sent over to Mrs. Hall's to stay. Elsie and Clover were to have gone too, but they begged so hard, and made so many promises of good behaviour, that finally Papa permitted them to remain. The dear little things stole about the house on tiptoe, as quietly as mice, whispering to each other, and waiting on Katy, who would have been lonely enough without them, for everybody else was absorbed in Aunt Izzie.

It was a confused, melancholy time. The three girls didn't know much about sickness, but Papa's grave face, and the hushed house, weighed upon their spirits, and they missed the children very much.

"Oh dear!" sighed Elsie. "How I wish Aunt Izzie would hurry and get well!"

"We'll be very good to her when she does, won't we?" said Clover. "I never mean to leave my goloshes in the hat-stand any more, because she doesn't like it. And I shall pick up the croquet balls and put them in the box every night."

"Yes," added Elsie, "so will I, when she gets well."

It never occurred to either of them that perhaps Aunt Izzie might not get well. Little people are apt to feel as if grown folks are so strong and so big, that nothing can possibly happen to them.

Katy was more anxious. Still she did not fairly realize the danger. So it came like a sudden and violent shock to her, when, one morning on waking up, she found old Mary crying quietly beside the bed, with her apron at her eyes. Aunt Izzie had died in the night!

All their kind, penitent thoughts of her; their resolutions to please—their plans for obeying her wishes and saving her trouble, were too late! For the first time, the three girls, sobbing in each other's arms, realized what a good friend Aunt Izzie had been to them. Her worrying ways were all forgotten now. They could only remember the many kind things she had done for them since they were little children. How they wished that they had never teased her, never said sharp words about her to each other! But it was no use to wish.

"What shall we do without Aunt Izzie?" thought Katy, as she cried herself to sleep that night. And the question came into her mind again and again, after the funeral was over and the little ones had come back from Mrs. Hall's, and things began to go on in their usual manner.

For several days she saw almost nothing of her father. Clover reported that he looked very tired, and scarcely said a word.

"Did Papa eat any dinner?" asked Katy, one afternoon.

"Not much. He said he wasn't hungry. And Mrs. Jackson's boy came for him before we were through."

"0 dear!" sighed Katy; "I do hope *he* isn't going to be ill. How it rains! Clover, I wish you'd run down and get out his slippers and put them by the fire to warm. Oh, and ask Debby to make some cream toast for tea. Papa likes cream-toast."

After tea, Dr. Carr came upstairs to sit a while in Katy's room. He often did so, but this was the first time since Aunt Izzie's death.

Katy studied his face anxiously. It seemed to her that it had grown older of late, and there was a sad look upon it, which made her heart ache. She longed to do something for him, but all she could do was to poke the fire bright, and then to possess herself of his hand, and stroke it gently with both hers. It wasn't much, to be sure, but I think Papa liked it.

"What have you been about all day?" he asked.

"Oh, nothing much!" said Katy. "I studied my French lesson this morning. And after school Elsie and John brought in their patchwork, and we had a 'Bee'. That's all."

"I've been thinking how we are to manage about the housekeeping," said Dr. Carr. "Of course we shall have to get somebody to come and take charge. But it isn't easy to find just the right person. Mrs. Hall knows of a woman who might do, but she is out West just now, and it will be a week or two before we can hear from her. Do you think you can get on as you are for a few days?"

"Oh, Papa!" cried Katy, in dismay, "must we have anybody?"

"Why, how do you suppose we were going to arrange it? Clover is much too young for a house-keeper. And besides, she is at school all day."

"I don't know—I hadn't thought about it," said Katy, in a perplexed tone.

But she did think about it—all that evening, and the first thing when she woke in the morning.

139

"Papa," she said, the next time she got him to herself, "I've been thinking over what you were saying last night, about getting somebody to keep the house, you know. And I wish you wouldn't. I wish you would let *me* try. Really and truly, I think I could manage."

"But how?" asked Dr. Carr, much surprised. "I really don't see. If you were well and strong, perhaps—but even then you would be pretty young for such a charge, Katy."

"I shall be fourteen in two weeks," said Katy, drawing herself up in her chair as straight as she could. "And if I *were* well, Papa, I should be going to school, you know, and then of course I couldn't. No, I'll tell you my plan. I've been thinking about it all day. Debbie and Bridget have been with us so long that they know all Aunt Izzie's ways, and they're such good women, that all they want is just to be told a little now and then. Now, why couldn't they come up to me when anything is wanted—just as well as to have me go down to them? Clover and old Mary will keep watch, you know, and see if anything is wrong. And you wouldn't mind if things were a little crooked just at first, would you? Because, you know, I should be learning all the time. Do let me try! It will be so nice to have something to think about as I sit up here alone, so much better than having a stranger in the house who doesn't know the children or anything. I am sure it will make me happier. Please say 'Yes', Papa— please do!"

"It's too much for you, a great deal too much," replied Dr. Carr. But it was not easy to resist Katy's "Please! Please!" and after a while it ended with:

"Well, darling, you may try, though I am doubtful as to the result of the experiment. I will tell Mrs. Hall to put off writing to Wisconsin for a month, and we will see."

"Poor child, anything to take her thoughts off

140

herself!" he muttered, as he walked downstairs. "She'll be glad enough to give the thing up by the end of a month."

But Papa was mistaken. At the end of a month Katy was eager to go on. So he said, "Very well—she might try it till spring."

It was not such hard work as it sounds. Katy had plenty of quiet thinking-time for one thing. The children were at school all day, and few visitors came to interrupt her, so she could plan out her hours and keep to the plans. That is a great help to a house-keeper.

Then Aunt Izzie's regular, punctual ways were so well understood by the servants that the house seemed almost to keep itself. As Katy had said, all Debby and Bridget needed was a little "telling" now and then.

As soon as breakfast was over, and the dishes were washed and put away, Debbie would tie on a clean apron, and come upstairs for orders. At first Katy thought this great fun. But after ordering dinner a good many times, it began to grow tiresome. She never saw the dishes after they were cooked; and, being inexperienced, it seemed impossible to think of things enough to make a variety.

"Let me see, there is roast beef—leg of mutton—boiled chicken," she would say, counting on her fingers; "roast beef—leg of mutton—boiled chicken. Debby, you might roast the chickens. Dear!—I wish somebody would invent a new animal! Where all the things to eat are gone to, I can't imagine!"

Then Katy would send for every recipe-book in the house, and pore over them by the hour, till her appetite was as completely gone as if she had swallowed twenty dinners. Poor Debby learned to dread these books. She would stand by the door with her pleasant red face drawn up into a pucker, while Katy read aloud some impossible-sounding rule.

"This looks as if it were delicious, Debby, I wish you'd try it: 'Take a gallon of oysters, a pint of beef stock, sixteen soda biscuits, the juice of two lemons, four cloves, a glass of white wine, a sprig of marjoram, a sprig of thyme, a sprig of bay, a sliced shallot—'"

"Please, Miss Katy, what's them?"

"Oh, don't you know, Debby? It must be something quite common, for it's in almost all the recipes."

"No, Miss Katy, I never heard tell of it before. Miss Carr never gave me no 'shell-outs' at all at all!"

"Dear me, how provoking!" Katy would cry, flapping over the leaves of her book. "Then we must try something else."

Poor Debby! If she hadn't loved Katy so dearly, I think her patience must have given way. But she bore her trials meekly, except for an occasional grumble when alone with Bridget. Dr. Carr had to eat a great many queer things in those days. But he didn't mind, and as for the children, they enjoyed it. Dinner time became quite exciting, when nobody could tell exactly what any dish on the table was made of. Dorry, who was a sort of Dr. Livingstone where strange articles of food were concerned, usually made the first experiment, and if he said that it was good, the rest followed suit.

After a while Katy grew wiser. She ceased teasing Debby to try new things, and the Carr family went back to plain roast and boiled, much to the advantage of all concerned. But then another series of experiments began. Katy got hold of a book upon "The Stomach", and was seized with a rage for wholesome food. She entreated Clover and the other children to give up sugar, and butter, and gravy, and pudding-sauce, and buckwheat cakes, and pies, and almost everything else that they particularly liked. Boiled rice seemed to her the most sensible dessert, and she kept the family on it until finally John and Dorry started a rebellion, and Dr. Carr was forced to interfere.

"My dear, you are overdoing it sadly," he said, as Katy opened her book and prepared to explain her views. "I am glad to have the children eat simple food—but really, boiled rice five times in a week is too much."

Katy sighed, but submitted. Later, as the spring came on, she had a fit of over-anxiousness, and was always sending Clover down to ask Debby if her bread was not burning, or if she was sure that the pickles were not fermenting in their jars? She also fidgeted the children about wearing overshoes, and keeping on their coats, and behaved altogether as if the cares of the world were on her shoulders.

But all these were but the natural mistakes of a beginner. Katy was too much in earnest not to improve. Month by month she learned how to manage a little better, and a little better still. Matters went on more smoothly. Her cares ceased to fret her. Dr. Carr, watching the increasing brightness of her face and manner, felt that the experiment was a success. Nothing more was said about "somebody else", and Katy, sitting upstairs in her big chair, held the threads of the house firmly in her hands.

CHAPTER TWELVE

TWO YEARS AFTERWARDS

It was a pleasant morning in early June. A warm wind was rustling the trees, which were covered thickly with half-opened leaves, and looked like fountains of green spray thrown high into the air. Dr. Carr's front door stood wide open. Through the parlour window came the sound of piano practice, and on the steps, under the budding roses, sat a small figure, busily sewing.

This was Clover, little Clover still, though more than two years had passed since we saw her last, and she was now over fourteen. Clover was never intended to be tall. Her eyes were as blue and sweet as ever, and her apple-blossom cheeks as pink. But the brown pigtails were pinned up into a round knot, and the childish face had gained almost a womanly look. Old Mary declared that Miss Clover was getting quite young ladyfied, and "Miss Clover" was quite aware of the fact, and mightily pleased with it. It delighted her to turn up her hair, and she was very particular about having her dresses made to come below the tops of her boots. She had also left off rules, and wore narrow collars instead, and little cuffs with sleeve-buttons to fasten them. These sleeve-buttons, which were a present from Cousin Helen, Clover liked best of all her things. Papa said that he was sure she took them to bed with her, but of course that was only a joke, though she certainly was never seen without them in the day time. She glanced frequently at these beloved buttons as she sat sewing, and every now and then laid down her work to twist them into a better position, or give them an affectionate pat with her forefinger.

Pretty soon the side gate swung open, and Philly came round the corner of the house. He had grown into a big boy. All his pretty baby curls were cut off, and his frocks had given place to jacket and trousers. In his hand he held something. What, Clover could not see.

"What's that?" she said, as he reached the steps.

"I'm going upstairs to ask Katy if these are ripe," replied Phil, exhibiting some currants faintly streaked with red.

"Why, of course they're not ripe!" said Clover, putting one into her mouth. "Can't you tell by the taste? They're as green as can be."

"I don't care; if Katy says they're ripe I shall eat them," answered Phil defiantly, marching into the house.

"What did Philly want?" asked Elsie, opening the parlour door as Phil went upstairs.

"Only to know if the currants are ripe enough to eat."

"How particular he always is about asking now" said Elsie. "He's afraid of another dose of salts."

"I should think he would be," replied Clover, laughing. "Johnnie says she never was so scared in her life as when Papa called them, and they looked up, and saw him standing there with the bottle in one hand and a spoon in the other!"

"Yes," went on Elsie; "and you know Dorry held his in his mouth for ever so long, and then went round the corner of the house and spat it out! Papa said he had a good mind to make him take another spoonful, but he remembered that after all Dorry had the bad taste a great deal longer than the others, so he didn't. I think it was an *awful* punishment, don't you?"

"Yes, but it was a good one, for none of them have ever touched the green gooseberries since. Have you got through practising? It doesn't seem like an hour yet."

"Oh, it isn't—it's only twenty-five minutes. But Katy told me not to sit more than half an hour at a time without getting up and running round to rest. I'm going to walk twice down to the gate, and twice back. I promised her I would." And Elsie set off, clapping her hands briskly before and behind her as she walked.

"Why, what is Bridget doing in Papa's room?" she asked, as she came back the second time. "She's flapping things out of the window. Are the servants up there? I thought they were cleaning the dining-room."

"They're doing both. Katy said it was such a good chance, having Papa away, that she would have both the carpets taken up at once. There isn't going to be any dinner today, only just bread-and-butter, and milk, and cold ham, up in Katy's room, because Debby is helping too, so as to get through and save Papa all the fuss. And see," exhibiting her sewing, "Katy's making a new cover for Papa's pin-cushion, and I'm hemming the rule to go round it."

"How nicely you hem!" said Elsie. "I wish I had something for Papa's room too. There's my washstand mats—but the one for the soap-dish isn't finished. Do you suppose, if Katy would excuse me from the rest of my practising, I could get it done? I've a great mind to go and ask her."

"There's her bell!" said Clover, as a little tinkle sounded upstairs; "I'll ask her, if you like."

"No, let me go. I'll see what she wants." But Clover was already half-way across the hall, and the two girls ran up side by side. There was often a little strife between them as to which should answer Katy's bell. Both liked to wait on her so much.

Katy came to meet them as they entered. Not on her feet: that, alas! was still only a far-off possibility; but in a chair with large wheels, with which she was rolling herself across he room.

This chair was a great comfort to her. Sitting in it, she could get to her closet and her bureau drawers, and help herself to what she wanted without troubling anybody. It was only lately that she had been able to use it. Dr. Carr considered her doing so as a hopeful sign, but he had never told Katy this. She had grown accustomed to her invalid life at last, and was cheerful in it, and he thought it unwise to make her restless, by exciting hopes which might after all end in fresh disappointment.

She met the girls with a bright smile as they came in, and said:

"Oh, Clover, it was you I rang for! I am troubled for fear Bridget will meddle with the things on Papa's table. You now he likes them to be left just so. Will you please go and remind her that she is not to touch them at all? After the carpet is put down, I want you to dust the table, so as to be sure that everything is put back in the same place. Will you?"

"Of course I will!" said Clover, who was a born house-wife, and dearly loved to act as Katy's prime minister. "Shan't I fetch you the pin-cushion too, while I'm there?"

"Oh, yes, please do! I want to measure."

"Katy," said Elsie, "those mats of mine are almost done, and I would like to finish them and put them on Papa's washstand before he comes back. Mayn't I stop practising now, and bring my crochet up here instead?"

"Will there be plenty of time to learn the new exercise before Miss Phillips comes, if you do?"

147

"I think so, plenty. She doesn't come till Friday, you know."

"Well then, it seems to me that you might just as well as not. And, Elsie dear, run into Papa's room first and bring me the drawer out of his table. I want to put that in order myself."

Elsie went cheerfully. She laid the drawer across Katy's lap, and Katy began to dust and arrange the contents. Pretty soon Clover joined them.

"Here's the cushion," she said. "Now we'll have a nice quiet time all by ourselves, won't we? I like this sort of a day, when nobody comes in to interrupt us."

Somebody tapped at the door as she spoke. Katy called out "Come in!" And in marched a tall, broad-shouldered lad, with a solemn, sensible face, and a little clock carried carefully in both his hands. This was Dorry. He has grown and improved very much since we saw him last, and is turning out clever in several ways. Among the rest, he has developed a strong turn for mechanics.

"Here's your clock, Katy," he said. "I've got it mended so that it strikes all right. Only you must be careful not to hit the striker when you start the pendulum."

"Have you really?" said Katy. "Why, Dorry, you're a genius! I'm ever so much obliged."

"It's four minutes to eleven now," went on Dorry. "So it'll strike pretty soon. I think I'd better stay and hear it, so as to be sure that it is right. That is," he added politely, "unless you're busy and would rather not."

"I'm never too busy to want you, old fellow," said Katy, stroking his arm. "Here, this drawer is arranged now. Won't you carry it into Papa's room and put it back into the table? Your hands are stronger than Elsie's."

148

Dorry looked gratified. When he came back the clock was just beginning to strike.

"There!" he exclaimed. "That's splendid, isn't it?"

But alas! the clock did not stop at eleven. It went on—Twelve, Thirteen, Fourteen, Fifteen, Sixteen!

"Dear me!" said Clover. "What does all this mean? It must be the day after tomorrow, at least."

Dorry stared with open mouth at the clock, which was still striking as though it would split its sides. Elsie, screaming with laughter, kept count.

"Thirty, Thirty-one—Oh, Dorry! Thirty-two! Thirty-three! Thirty-four!"

"You've bewitched it, Dorry!" said Katy, as much entertained as the rest.

Then they all began counting. Dorry seized the clock—shook it, slapped it, turned it upside-down. But still the sharp, vibrating sounds continued, as if the clock, having got its own way for once, meant to go on till it was tired out.

At last, at the one-hundred-and-thirtieth stroke, it suddenly ceased; and Dorry, with a red, amazed countenance, faced the laughing company.

"It's very queer," he said, "but I'm sure it's not because of anything I did. I can mend it, though, if you'll let me try again. May I, Katy? I'll promise not to hurt it."

For a moment Katy hesitated. Clover pulled her sleeve, and whispered "Don't!" Then seeing the mortification on Dorry's face, she made up her mind.

"Yes, take it, Dorry. I'm sure you'll be careful. But if I were you, I'd carry it down to Wetherell's first of all, and talk it over with them. Together you could hit on just the right thing. Don't you think so?"

"Perhaps," said Dorry; "yes, I think I will." Then he departed with the clock under his arm, while Clover called after him teasingly, "Lunch at 132 o'clock, don't forget!"

"No, I won't!" said Dorry. Two years before he would not have borne to be laughed at so good-naturedly.

"How could you let him take your clock again?" said Clover, as soon as the door was shut. "He'll spoil it. And you think so much of it."

"I thought he would feel mortified if I didn't let him try," replied Katy quietly; "I don't believe he'll hurt it. Wetherell's man likes Dorry, and he'll show him what to do."

"You were very good to do it," responded Clover; "but if it had been mine I don't think I could."

Just then the door flew open, and Johnnie rushed in, two years taller, but otherwise looking exactly as she used to do.

"Oh, Katy!" she gasped. "Won't you please tell Philly not to wash the chickens in the rain-water tub? He's put in every one of Speckle's, and is just beginning on Dame Durden's. I'm afraid one little yellow one is dead already——"

"Why, he mustn't—of course he mustn't!" said Katy. "What made him think of such a thing?"

"He says they're dirty, because they've just come out of eggshells! And he insists that the yellow on them is yolk of egg. I told him it wasn't, but he wouldn't listen to me." And Johnnie wrung her hands.

"Clover," cried Katy, "won't you run down and ask Philly to come up to me? Speak pleasantly, you know."

"I spoke pleasantly—really pleasantly, but it wasn't any use," said Johnnie, on whom the wrongs to the chicks had evidently made a deep impression.

"What a mischief Phil is getting to be!" said Elsie. "Papa says his name ought to be 'Pickle'."

150

"Pickles turn out very nice sometimes, you know," replied Katy, laughing.

Pretty soon Philly came up, escorted by Clover. He looked a little defiant, but Katy understood how to manage him. She lifted him into her lap, which, big boy as he was, he liked extremely; and talked to him so affectionately about the poor little shivering chicks that his heart was quite melted.

"I didn't mean to hurt them really and truly," he said; "but they were all dirty and yellow—with egg, you know, and I thought you'd like me to clean them up."

"But that wasn't egg, Philly—it was dear little clean feathers, like a canary-bird's wings."

"Was it?"

"Yes. And now the chickies are as cold and forlorn as you would feel if you tumbled into a pond and nobody gave you any dry clothes. Don't you think you ought to go and warm them?"

"How?"

"Well—in your hands, very gently. And then I would let them run round in the sun."

"I will," said Philly, getting down from her lap. "Only kiss me first, because I didn't mean to, you know." Philly was very fond of Katy. Miss Petingill said it was wonderful to see how that child let himself be managed. But I think the secret was that Katy didn't "manage", but tried to be always kind and loving, and considerate of Phil's feelings.

Before the echo of Phil's boots had fairly died away on the stairs, old Mary put her head into the door. There was a distressed expression on her face.

"Miss Katy," she said, "I wish *you'd* speak to Alexander about putting the woodshed in order. I don't think you know how bad it looks."

"I don't suppose I do," said Katy, smiling, and then

sighing. She had never seen the woodshed since the day of her fall from the swing. "Never mind, Mary, I'll talk to Alexander about it, and he shall make it all nice."

Mary trotted downstairs satisfied. But in the course of a few minutes she was up again.

"There's a man come with a box of soap, Miss Katy, and here's the bill. He says it's restated."

It took Katy a little time to find her purse, and then she wanted her pencil and account book, and Elsie had to move from her seat at the table.

"Oh dear!" she said, "I wish people wouldn't keep coming and interrupting us. Who'll be the next. I wonder?"

She was not left to wonder long. Almost as she spoke there was another knock at the door.

"Come in!" said Katy, rather wearily. The door opened.

"Shall I?" said a voice. There was a rustle of skirts, a clatter of boot-heels, and Imogen Clark swept into the room. Katy could not think who it was, at first. She had not seen Imogen for almost two years.

"I found the front door open," exclaimed Imogen, in her high-pitched voice, "and as nobody seemed to hear when I rang the bell, I ventured to come right upstairs. I hope I'm not interrupting anything private?"

"Not at all," said Katy, politely. "Elsie dear, move up that low chair, please. Do sit down, Imogen. I'm sorry nobody answered your ring; but the servants are house-cleaning today, and I suppose they didn't hear."

So Imogen sat down and began to rattle on in her usual manner, while Elsie, from behind Katy's chair, took a wide-awake survey of her dress. It was of cheap material, but very gorgeously made and trimmed, with flounces and puffs; and Imogen wore a jet necklace and

152

long black ear-rings, which jingled and clicked when she waved her head about. She still had the little round curls stuck on to her cheeks, and Elsie wondered anew what kept them in their places.

By and by the object of Imogen's visit came out. She had called to say goodbye. The Clark family were all going back to Jacksonville to live.

"Did you ever see the Brigand again?" asked Clover, who had never forgotten that eventful tale told in the parlour.

"Yes," replied Imogen, "several times. And I get letters from him quite often. He writes *beau*tiful letters. I wish I had one with me, so that I could read you a little bit. You would enjoy it, I know. Let me see— perhaps I have." And she put her hand into her pocket. Sure enough, there *was* a letter. Clover couldn't help suspecting that Imogen knew it all the time.

The Brigand seemed to write a bold, black hand, and his notepaper and envelope was just like anybody else's. But perhaps his band had surprised a pedlar with a box of stationery. "Let me see," said Imogen, running her eye down the page. "'Adored Imogen'— *that* wouldn't interest you—hm, hm, hm—ah, here's something! 'I took dinner at the Rock House on Christmas. It was lonesome without you. I had roast turkey, roast goose, roast beef, mince pie, plum pudding, and nuts and raisins. A pretty good dinner, was it not? But nothing tastes first-rate when friends are away.'"

Katy and Clover stared, as well they might. Such language from a Brigand!

"'John Billings has bought a new horse'," continued Imogen; "hm, hm, hm—him. I don't think there is anything else you'd care about. Oh, yes! just here, at the end, is some poetry:

    "'Come, little dove, with azure wing,
    And brood upon my breast.'"

    "That's sweet, isn't it?"

    "Hasn't he reformed?" said Clover. "He writes as if
he had."

    "Reformed!" cried Imogen, with a toss of the jingling
earrings. "He was always just as good as he could be."

    There was nothing to be said in reply to this. Katy
felt her lips twitch, and for fear she should be rude,
and laugh out, she began to talk as fast as she could
about something else. All the time she found herself
taking measure of Imogen, and thinking—"Did I ever
really like her? How queer! Oh, what a wise man Papa
is!"

    Imogen stayed half an hour. Then she took her leave.

    "She never asked how you were!" cried Elsie, indig-
nantly. "I noticed, and she didn't—not once."

    "Oh, well—I suppose she forgot. We were talking
about her, not about me," replied Katy.

    The little group settled down again to their work.
This time half an hour went by without any more inter-
ruptions. Then the door-bell rang, and Bridget, with a
disturbed face, came upstairs.

    "Miss Katy," she said, "it's old Mr. Worrett, and I
reckon she's come to spend the day, for she's brought
her bag. Whatever shall I tell her?"

    Katy looked dismayed. "Oh dear!" she said. "How
unlucky! What can we do?"

    Mrs. Worrett was an old friend of Aunt Izzie's, who
lived in the country, about six miles from Burnet, and
was in the habit of coming to Dr. Carr's for lunch, on
days when shopping or other business brought her into
town. This did not occur often; and, as it happened,
Katy had never had to entertain her before.

"Tell her you're busy, and can't see her," suggested Bridget; "there's no dinner nor nothing, you know."

The Katy of two years ago would probably have jumped at this idea. But the Katy of today was more considerate.

"N-o," she said; "I don't like to do that. We must just make the best of it, Bridget. Run down, Clover, dear, that's a good girl, and tell Mrs. Worrett that the dining-room is all in confusion, but that we're going to have lunch here, and, after she's rested, I should be glad to have her come up. And, oh, Clover! give her a fan the first thing. She'll be *so* hot. Bridget, you can bring up the luncheon just the same; only, take out some canned peaches, by way of a dessert, and make Mrs. Worrett a cup of tea. She drinks tea always, I believe.

"I can't bear to send the poor old lady away when she has come so far," she explained to Elsie, after the others were gone. "Pull the rocking-chair a little this way, Elsie. And, oh! push all those little chairs back against the wall. Mrs. Worrett broke one the last time she was here—don't you recollect?"

It took some time to cool Mrs. Worrett off, so nearly twenty minutes passed before a heavy, creaking step on the stairs announced that the guest was on her way up. Elsie began to giggle. Mrs. Worrett always made her giggle. Katy had just time to give her a warning glance before the door opened.

Mrs. Worrett was the most enormously fat person ever seen. Nobody dared to guess how much she weighed, but she *looked* as if it might be a thousand pounds. Her face was extremely red. In the coldest weather she appeared hot, and on a mild day she seemed absolutely ready to melt. Her bonnet strings were flying loose as she came in, and she fanned herself all the way across the room, which shook as she walked.

"Well, my dear," she said, as she plumped herself into the rocking-chair, "and how do you do?"

"Very well, thank you," replied Katy, thinking that she never saw Mrs. Worrett look half so fat before, and wondering how she *was* to entertain her.

"And how's your Papa?" inquired Mrs. Worrett.

Katy answered politely, and then asked after Mrs. Worret's own health.

"Well, I'm so's to be round," was the reply, which had the effect of sending Elsie off into a fit of convulsive laughter behind Katy's chair.

"I had business at the bank," continued the visitor, "and I thought, while I was about it, I'd step up to Miss Petingill's and see if I couldn't get her to come and let out my black silk. It was made some time ago, and I seem to have got stouter since then, for I can't make the hooks and eyes meet at all. But when I got there she was out, so I'd my walk for nothing. Do you know where she's sewing now?"

"No," said Katy, feeling her chair shake, and keeping her own countenance with difficulty; "she was here for three days last week to make Johnnie a school dress. But I haven't heard anything about her since. Elsie, will you run down-stairs, and ask Bridget to bring a—a—a glass of iced water for Mrs. Worrett? She looks warm after her walk."

Elsie, dreadfully ashamed, made a bolt from the room, and hid herself in the hall closet to have her laugh out. She came back after a while with a perfectly straight face. Luncheon was brought up. Mrs. Worrett made a good meal, and seemed to enjoy everything. She was so comfortable that she never stirred till four o'clock! Oh, how long that afternoon did seem to the poor girls, sitting there and trying to think of something to say to their vast visitor!

At last Mrs. Worrett got out of her chair and prepared to depart.

"Well," she said, tying her bonnet strings, "I've had a good rest, and feel all the better for it. Aren't some of you young folks coming out to see me one of these days? I'd like to have you, first-rate, if you will. It is not every girl would know how to take care of a fat old woman, and make her feel at home, as you have made me, Katy. I wish your aunt could see you all as you are now. She'd be very pleased, I know that."

Somehow this sentence rang pleasantly in Katy's ears.

"Ah, don't laugh at her!" she said, later in the evening, when the children, after their tea in the clean, fresh-smelling dining-room, were come up to sit with her, and Cecy, in her pretty pink lawn and white shawl, had dropped in to spend an hour or two. "She's a really kind old woman, and I don't like to hear you. It isn't her fault that she's fat. And Aunt Izzie was fond of her, you know. It is doing something for her when we can show a little attention to one of her friends. I was sorry when she came; but now it's over, I'm glad."

"It feels so nice when it stops aching," quoted Elsie, mischievously, while Cecy whispered to Clover:

"Isn't Katy sweet?"

"Isn't she!" replied Clover. "I wish I was half so good. Sometimes I think I shall really be sorry if she ever gets well. She's such a dear old darling to us all, sitting there in her chair, that it wouldn't seem so nice to have her anywhere else. But, then, I know it's horrid of me. And I don't believe she'd be different or grow horrid, like some of the girls, even if she were well."

"Of course she wouldn't!" replied Cecy.

CHAPTER THIRTEEN

AT LAST

It was about six weeks after this, that one day when Clover and Elsie were busy downstairs, they were startled by the sound of Katy's bell ringing in a sudden and agitated manner. Both ran up two steps at a time, to see what was wanted.

Katy sat in her chair, looking very much flushed and excited.

"Oh, girls!" she exclaimed. "What do you think? I stood up!"

"What?" cried Clover and Elsie.

"I really did! I stood up on my feet! by myself!"

The others were too much astonished to speak, so Katy went on explaining.

"It was all at once, you see. Suddenly I had the feeling that if I tried I could, and almost before I thought, I *did* try, and there I was, up and out of the chair. Only I kept hold of the arm all the time! I don't know how I got back, I was so frightened. Oh, girls!"— and Katy buried her face in her hands.

"Do you think I shall ever be able to do it again?" she asked, looking up with wet eyes.

"Why, of course you will!" said Clover; while Elsie danced about, crying out anxiously: "Be careful! Do be careful!"

Katy tried, but the spring was gone. She could not move out of the chair at all. She began to wonder if she had dreamed the whole thing.

But next day, when Clover happened to be in the

room, she heard a sudden exclamation, and turning, there stood Katy, absolutely on her feet.

"Papa! Papa!" shrieked Clover, rushing downstairs. "Dorry, John, Elsie—come! Come and see!"

Papa was out, but all the rest crowded up at once. This time Katy found no trouble in "doing it again".

It seemed as if her will had been asleep; and now that it had awoken the limbs recognized its orders and obeyed them.

When Papa came in he was as much excited as any of the children. He walked round and round the chair, questioning Katy and making her stand up and sit down.

"Am I really going to get well?" she asked, almost in a whisper.

"Yes, my love, I think you are," replied Dr. Carr, seizing Phil and giving him a toss into the air. None of the children had ever before seen Papa behave so like a boy. But pretty soon, noticing Katy's burning cheeks and excited eyes, he calmed himself, sent the others all away, and sat down to soothe and quiet her with gentle words.

"I think it is coming, my darling," he said, "but it will take time, and you must have a great deal of patience. After being such a good child all these years, I am sure you won't fail now. Remember, any imprudence will put you back. You must be content to gain very little at a time. There is no royal road to walking any more than there is to learning. Every baby finds that out."

"Oh, Papa!" said Katy. "It's no matter if it takes a year—if only I get well at last."

How happy she was that night—too happy to sleep! Papa noticed the dark circles under her eyes in the morning, and shook his head.

"You *must* be careful," he told her, "or you will be laid up again. A course of fever would put you back for years."

Katy knew Papa was right, and she *was* careful, though it was by no means easy to be so with that new life tingling in every limb. Her progress was slow, as Dr. Carr had predicted. At first she only stood on her feet a few seconds, then a minute, then five minutes, holding tightly all the while by the chair. Next she ventured to let go the chair, and stand alone. After that she began to walk a step at a time, pushing a chair before her, as children do when they are learning the use of their feet. Clover and Elsie hovered about her as she moved, like anxious mammas. It was droll, and a little pitiful, to see tall Katy with her feeble, unsteady progress, and the active figures of the little sisters following her protectingly. But Katy did not consider it either droll or pitiful; to her it was simply delightful— the most delightful thing possible. No baby of a year old was ever prouder of his first steps than she.

Gradually she grew adventurous, and ventured on a bolder flight. Clover, running upstairs one day to her own room, stood transfixed at the sight of Katy sitting there, flushed, panting, but enjoying the surprise she caused.

"You see," she explained in an apologizing tone, "I was seized with a desire to explore. It is such a time since I saw any room but my own! But, oh dear, how long that hall is! I had forgotten it could be so long. I shall have to take a good rest before I go back."

Katy did take a good rest, but she was very tired next day. The experiment, however, did no harm. In the course of two or three weeks she was able to walk all over the second storey.

This was a great enjoyment. It was like reading an

interesting book to see all the new things, and the little changes. She was for ever wondering over something.

"Why, Dorry," she would say, "what a pretty bookshelf! When did you get it?"

"That old thing! Why, I've had it two years. Didn't I ever tell you about it?"

"Perhaps you did," Katy would reply, "but, you see, I never *saw* it before, so it made no impression."

By the end of August she was growing so strong that she began to talk about going downstairs. But Papa said, "Wait".

"It will tire you much more than walking about on a level," he explained; "you had better put it off a little while—till you are quite sure of your feet."

"I think so too," said Clover; "and besides, I want to have the house all put in order and made nice, before your sharp eyes see it, Mrs. Housekeeper. Oh, I'll tell you! Such a beautiful idea has come into my head! You shall find a day to come down, Katy, and we'll be all ready for you, and have a 'celebration' among ourselves. That would be just lovely! How soon may she, Papa?"

"Well, in ten days, I should say, it might be safe."

"Ten days! That would bring it to the seventh of September won't it?" said Katy. "Then, Papa, if I may, I'll come down for the first time on the eighth. It was Mamma's birthday, you know," she added in a lower voice.

So it was settled. "How delicious!" cried Clover, skipping about and clapping her hands; "I never, never, never *did* hear of anything so perfectly lovely. Papa, when are you coming downstairs? I want to speak to you *dreadfully*."

"Just at once—rather than have my coat-tails pulled off," answered Dr. Carr, laughing, and they went away

161

together. Katy sat looking out of the window in a peaceful, happy mood.

"Oh!" she thought. "Can it really be? Is School going to 'let out', just as Cousin Helen's hymn said? Am I going to

'Bid a sweet goodbye to Pain'?

But there was Love in the Pain. I see it now. How good the dear Teacher has been to me!"

Clover seemed to be very busy all the rest of that week. She was "having windows washed," she said; but this explanation hardly accounted for her long absences, and the mysterious exultation on her face, not to mention certain sounds of hammering and sawing which came from down-stairs. The other children had evidently been warned to say nothing; for once or twice Philly broke out with, "Oh, Katy!" and then hushed himself up, saying, "I almost forgot!" Katy grew very curious. But she saw that the secret, whatever it was, gave immense satisfaction to everybody except herself; so, though she longed to know, she concluded not to spoil the fun by asking any questions.

At last it wanted but a day of the important occasion.

"See," said Katy, as Clover came into the room a little before tea time. "Miss Petingill has brought home my new dress. "I'm going to wear it for the first time to go downstairs in."

"How pretty!" said Clover, examining the dress, which was a soft, dove-coloured cashmere, trimmed with ribbon of the same shade. "But, Katy, I came up to shut your door. Bridget's going to sweep the hall, and I don't want the dust to fly in, because your room was brushed this morning, you know."

"What a queer time to sweep a hall!" said Katy,

wonderingly. "Why don't you make her wait till morning?"

"Oh, she can't! There are—she has—I mean there will be other things for her to do tomorrow. It's a great deal more convenient that she should do it now. Don't worry, Katy, darling, but just keep your door shut. You will, won't you? Promise me!"

"Very well," said Katy, more and more amazed, but yielding to Clover's eagerness. "I'll keep it shut." Her curiosity was excited. She took a book and tried to read, but the letters danced up and down before her eyes, and she couldn't help listening. Bridget was making a most ostentatious noise with her broom, but through it all Katy seemed to hear other sounds—feet on the stairs, doors opening and shutting—once, a stifled giggle. How queer it all was!

"Never mind," she said, resolutely stopping her ears, "I shall know all about it tomorrow."

Tomorrow dawned fresh and fair—the very ideal of a September day.

"Katy," said Clover, as she came in from the garden with her hands full of flowers! "that dress of yours is sweet. You never looked so nice before in your life!" And she stuck a beautiful carnation pink under Katy's breast-pin, and fastened another in her hair.

"There!" she said. "Now you're adorned. Papa is coming up in a few minutes to take you down."

Just then Elsie and Johnnie came in. They had on their best frocks. So had Clover. It was evidently a festival day to all the house. Cecy followed, invited over for the special purpose of seeing Katy walk downstairs. She too had on a new frock.

"How fine we are!" said Clover, as she remarked this magnificence. "Turn round, Cecy—a panier, I do declare—and a sash! You are getting awfully grown-up, Miss Hall."

"None of us will ever be so 'grown-up' as Katy," said Cecy, laughing. And now Papa appeared. Very slowly they all went downstairs, Katy leaning on Papa, with Dorry on her other side, and the girls behind, while Philly clattered ahead. And there were Debby and Bridget and Alexander, peeping out of the kitchen door to watch her, and dear old Mary with her apron at her eyes, crying for joy.

"Oh, the front door is open!" said Katy, in a delighted-tone. "How nice! And what a pretty oilcloth! That's new since I was here."

"Don't stop to look at *that*!" cried Philly, who seemed in a great hurry about something. "It isn't new. It's been there ever and ever so long! Come into the parlour instead."

"Yes," said Papa; "dinner isn't quite ready yet; you'll have time to rest a little after your walk downstairs. You have borne it admirably, Katy. Are you very tired?"

"Not a bit!" replied Katy, cheerfully. "I could do it alone, I think. Oh! The bookcase door has been mended. How nice it looks!"

"Don't wait, oh, don't wait!" repeated Phil, in an agony of impatience.

So they moved on. Papa opened the parlour door. Katy took one step into the room—then stopped. The colour flashed over her face, and she held on to the doorknob to support herself. What was it that she saw?

Not merely the room itself, with its fresh muslin curtains and vases of flowers. Nor even the wide, beautiful window which had been cut towards the sun, or the inviting little couch and table which stood there, evidently for her.

No, there was something else! The sofa was pulled

out, and there upon it, supported by pillows, her bright eyes turned to the door, lay—Cousin Helen! When she saw Katy she held out her arms.

Clover and Cecy agreed afterwards that they never were so frightened in their lives as at this moment; for Katy, forgetting her weakness, let go of Papa's arm, and absolutely *ran* towards the sofa. "Oh, Cousin Helen! dear, dear Cousin Helen!" she cried. Then she tumbled down by the sofa somehow, the two pairs of arms and the two faces met, and for a moment or two not a word more was heard from anybody.

"Isn't it a nice surprise?" shouted Philly, turning a somersault by way of relieving his feelings, while John and Dorry executed a sort of war dance round the sofa.

Phil's voice seemed to break the spell of silence, and a perfect hubbub of questions and exclamations began.

It appeared that this happy thought of getting Cousin Helen to the "Celebration", was Clover's. She it was who had proposed it to Papa, and made all the arrangements. And—artful puss!—she had set Bridget to sweep the hall, on purpose that Katy might not hear the noise of the arrival.

"Cousin Helen's going to stay three weeks this time—isn't that nice?" asked Elsie, while Clover anxiously questioned: "Are you sure that you didn't suspect? Not one bit? Not the least tiny, weeny mite?"

"No, indeed—not the least. How could I suspect anything so perfectly delightful?" And Katy gave Cousin Helen another rapturous kiss.

Such a short day as that seemed! There was so much to see, to ask about, to talk over, that the hours flew, and evening dropped upon them all like another great surprise.

Cousin Helen was perhaps the happiest of the party. Besides the pleasure of knowing Katy to be almost well again, she had the additional enjoyment of seeing for herself how many changes for the better had taken place, during the four years, among the little cousins she loved so much.

It was very interesting to watch them all. Elsie and Dorry seemed to her the most improved of the family. Elsie had quite lost her plaintive look and little injured tone, and was as bright and beaming a maiden of twelve as anyone could wish to see. Dorry's moody face had grown open and sensible, and his manners were good-humoured and obliging. He was still a sober boy, and not specially quick in catching an idea, but he promised to turn out a valuable man. And to him, as to all the other children, Katy was evidently the centre and the sun. They all revolved about her, and trusted her for everything. Cousin Helen looked on as Phil came in crying, after a hard tumble, and was consoled; as Johnnie whispered an important secret, and Elsie begged for help in her work. She saw Katy meet them all pleasantly and sweetly, without a bit of the dictatorial elder sister in her manner, and with none of her old, impetuous tone. And best of all, she saw the change in Katy's own face: the gentle expression of her eyes, the womanly look, the pleasant voice, the politeness, the tact in advising the others, without seeming to advise.

"Dear Katy," she said a day or two after her arrival, "this visit is a great pleasure to me—you can't think how great. It is such a contrast to the last I made, when you were so sick, and everybody so sad. Do you remember?"

"Indeed I do. And how good you were, and how you helped me. I shall never forget that."

"I'm glad. But what I could do was very little. You have been learning by yourself all this time. And, Katy

166

darling, I want to tell you how pleased I am to see how bravely you have worked your way up. I can perceive it in everything—in Papa, in the children, in yourself. You have won the place, which, you recollect, I once told you an invalid should try to gain, of being to everybody 'The Heart of the House'."

"Oh, Cousin Helen, don't!" said Katy, her eyes filling with sudden tears. "I haven't been brave. You can't think how badly I sometimes have behaved—how cross and ungrateful I am, and how stupid and slow. Every day I see things which ought to be done, and I don't do them. It's too delightful to have you praise me—but you mustn't. I don't deserve it."

But although she said she didn't deserve it, I think that Katy did!

CHAPTER FOURTEEN

CONIC SECTION

It was just after that happy visit of which I told that Elsie and John made their famous excursion to Conic Section; an excursion which neither of them ever forgot, and about which the family teased them for a long time afterwards.

The summer had been cool; but, as often happens after cool summers, the autumn proved unusually hot. It seemed as if the months had been playing a game, and had "changed places" all round; and as if September was determined to show that he knew how to make himself just as disagreeable as August, if only he chose to do so. All the last half of Cousin Helen's stay, the weather was excessively sultry. She felt it very much, though the children did all they could to make her comfortable, with shaded rooms, and iced water, and fans. Every evening the boys would wheel her sofa out on the porch, in hopes of coolness; but it was of no use: the evenings were as warm as the days, and the yellow dust hanging in the air made the sunshine look thick and hot. A few bright leaves appeared on the trees, but they were wrinkled, and of an ugly colour. Clover said she thought they had been boiled red like lobsters. Altogether, the month was a trying one, and the coming of October made little or no difference: still the dust continued, and the heat; and the wind, when it blew, had no refreshment in it, but seemed to have passed over some great furnace which had burned out of it all life and flavour.

In spite of this, however, it was wonderful to see how Katy gained and improved. Every day added to her powers. First she came down to dinner, then to breakfast. She sat on the porch in the afternoons; she poured the tea. It was like a miracle to the others, in the beginning, to watch her going about the house; but they got used to it surprisingly soon—one does to pleasant things. One person, however, never got used to it, never took it as a matter of course; and that was Katy herself. She could not run down-stairs, or out into the garden; she could not open the kitchen door to give an order, without a sense of gladness and exultation which was beyond words. The wider and more active life stimulated her in every way. Her cheeks grew round and pink, her eyes bright. Cousin Helen and Papa watched this change with indescribable pleasure; and Mrs. Worrett, who dropped in to

168

lunch one day, fairly screamed.with surprise at the sight of it.

"To think of it!" she cried. "Why, the last time I was here you looked as if you had took root in that chair of yours for the rest of your days, and here you are stepping about as lively as I be. Well, well! Wonders will never cease. It does my eyes good to see you, Katherine. I wish your poor aunt were here today; that I do. How pleased she'd be!"

It is doubtful whether Aunt Izzie would have been so pleased, for the lived-in look of the best parlour would have horrified her extremely; but Katy did not think of that just then. She was touched at the genuine kindness of Mrs. Worrett's voice, and took very willingly her offered kiss. Clover brought lemonade and grapes, and they all devoted themselves to making the poor lady comfortable. Just before she went away she said:

"How is it that I can't never get any of you to come out to Conic Section? I'm sure I've asked you often enough. There's Elsie, now, and John, they're just the age to enjoy being in the country. Why won't you send 'em out for a week? Johnnie can feed chickens, and chase 'em too, if she likes," she added, as Johnnie dashed just then into view, pursuing one of Phil's bantams round the house. "Tell her so, won't you, Katherine? There is lots of chickens on the farm. She can chase 'em from morning to night, if she's a mind to."

Katy thanked her, but she didn't think the children would care to go. She gave Johnnie the message, and then the whole matter passed out of her mind. She was surprised, a few days later, by having it brought up again by Elsie. The family were in low spirits that morning because of Cousin Helen's having just gone away, and Elsie was lying on the sofa, fanning herself with a great palm-leaf fan.

"Oh dear!" he sighed. "Do you suppose it's ever going to be cool again in this world? It does seem as if I couldn't bear it any longer."

"Aren't you well enough," inquired Katy, anxiously.

"Oh yes! well enough," replied Elsie. "It's only this horrid heat, and never going away to where it's cooler."

"I keep thinking about the country, and wishing I were there feeling the wind blow. I wonder if Papa wouldn't let me and John go to Conic Section, and see Mrs. Worrett. Do you think he would if you asked him?"

"But," said Katy, amazed, "Conic Section isn't exactly country, you know. It is just out of the city— only six miles from here. And Mrs. Worrett's house is close to the road, Papa said. Do you think you'd like it, dear? It can't be very much cooler than this."

"Oh yes, it can," rejoined Elsie, in a tone which was a little fretful. "It's quite near woods; Mrs Worrett told me so. Besides, it's always cooler on a farm. There's more room for the wind, and—oh, everything's pleasanter You can't think how tired I am of this hot house. Last night I hardly slept at all; and, when I did, I dreamed that I was a loaf of brown bread, and Debby was putting me into the oven to bake. It was a horrid dream. I was so glad to wake up. Won't you ask Papa if we may go, Katy?"

"Why, of course I will, if you wish it so much. Only—" Katy stopped and did not finish her sentence. A vision of fat Mrs. Worrett had risen before her, and she could not help doubting if Elsie would find the farm as pleasant as she expected. But sometimes the truest kindness is in giving people their own unwise way, and Elsie's eyes looked so wistful that Katy had no heart to argue or refuse.

Dr. Carr looked doubtful when the plan was proposed to him. "It's too hot," he said. "I don't believe the girls will like it."

"Oh yes, we will, Papa; indeed we will," pleaded Elsie and John, who had lingered near the door to learn the fate of their request.

Dr. Carr smiled at the imploring faces, but he looked a little quizzical. "Very well," he said, "you may go. Mr. Worrett is coming into town tomorrow, on some bank business. I'll send word by him; and in the afternoon, when it is cooler, Alexander can drive you out."

"Goody! Goody!" cried John, jumping up and down; while Elsie put her arms round Papa's neck and gave him a hug.

"And Thursday I'll send for you," he continued.

"But, Papa," expostulated Elsie, "that's only two days. Mrs. Worrett said a week."

"Yes, she said a week," chimed in John; "and she's got ever so many chickens, and I'm to feed them, and chase them about as much as I like. Only it's too hot to run much," she added reflectively.

"You won't really send for us on Thursday, will you, Papa?" urged Elsie, anxiously. "I'd like to stay ever and ever so long; but Mrs. Worrett said a week."

"I shall send on Thursday," repeated Dr. Carr, in a decided tone. Then, seeing that Elsie's lip was trembling, and her eyes were full of tears, he continued, "Don't look so woeful, Pussy. Alexander shall drive out for you; but if you want to stay longer, you may send him back with a note to say what day you would like to have him come again. Will that do?"

"Oh yes!" said Elsie, wiping her eyes; "that will do beautifully, Papa. Only, it seems such a pity that

Alexander should have to go twice when it's so hot; for we're perfectly sure to want to stay a week."

Papa only laughed, as he kissed her. All being settled, the children began to get ready. It was quite an excitement packing the bags, and deciding what to take and what not to take. Elsie grew bright and gay with the bustle. Just to think of being in the country—the cool green country— made her perfectly happy, she declared. The truth was, she was a little feverish and not quite well, and didn't know exactly how she felt or what she wanted.

The drive out was pleasant, except that Alexander upset John's gravity, and hurt Elsie's dignity very much, by inquiring, as they left the gate, "Do the little misses know where it is that they want to go?" Part of the way the road ran through woods. They were rather boggy woods; but the dense shade kept off the sun, and there was a spicy smell of evergreens and sweet fern. Elsie felt that the good time had fairly begun, and her spirits rose with every turn of the wheels.

By and by they left the woods, and came out again into the sunshine. The road was dusty, and so were the fields, and the ragged sheaves of corn-stalks, which dotted them here and there, looked dusty too. Piles of dusty red apples lay on the grass, under the orchard trees. Some cows, going down a lane towards their milking-shed, mooed in a dispirited and thirsty way, which made the children feel thirsty also.

"I want a drink of water awfully," said John. "Do you suppose it's much farther? How long will it be before we get to Mrs. Worrett's, Alexander?"

"'Most there, miss," replied Alexander laconically.

Elsie put her head out of the carriage, and looked eagerly round. Where was the delightful farm? She saw a big, pumpkin-coloured house by the roadside, a little

172

farther on; but surely that couldn't be it. Yes; Alexander drew up at the gate, and jumped down to lift them out. It really was! The surprise quite took away her breath.

She looked about. There were the woods, to be sure, but half a mile away across the fields. Near the house, there were no trees at all; only some lilac bushes at one side; there was no green grass either. A gravel path took up the whole of the narrow front yard; and, what with the blazing colour of the paint and the wide-awake look of the blindless windows, the house had somehow the air of standing on tiptoe and staring hard at something—the dust in the road, perhaps; for there seemed nothing else to stare at.

Elsie's heart sank indescribably, as she and John got very slowly out of the carryall, and Alexander, putting his arm over the fence, rapped loudly at the front door.

It was some minutes before the rap was answered. Then a heavy step was heard creaking through the hall, and somebody began fumbling at an obstinate bolt, which would not move. Next, a voice which they recognized as Mrs. Worrett's called: "Isaphiny! Isaphiny, come and see if you can open this door."

"How funny!" whispered Johnnie, beginning to giggle.

"Isaphiny" seemed to be upstairs; for presently they heard her running down, after which a fresh rattle began at the obstinate bolt. But still the door did not open, and at length Mrs. Worrett put her lips to the keyhole, and asked:

"Who is it?"

The voice sounded so hollow and ghostly, that Elsie jumped, as she answered: "It's I, Mrs. Worrett—Elsie Carr. And Johnnie's here too."

"Ts, ts, ts!" sounded from within, and then came a whispering; after which Mrs. Worrett put her mouth again to the keyhole, and called out: "Go round to the back, children. I can't make this door open anyway. It's all swelled up with the damp."

"Damp" whispered Johnnie, "Why, it hasn't rained since the third week in August; Papa said so yesterday."

"That's nothing, Miss Johnnie," put in Alexander, overhearing her. "Folks hereaway don't open their front doors much—only for weddings and funerals and such like. Very likely this has stood shut these five years. I know the last time I drove Miss Carr out, before she died, it was just so; and she had to go round to the back, as you're a-doing now."

John's eyes grew wide with wonder; but there was no time to say anything, for they had turned the corner of the house, and there was Mrs. Worrett waiting at the kitchen door to receive them. She looked fatter than ever, Elsie thought; but she kissed them both, and said she was very glad to see a Carr in her house at last. "It was too bad," she went on, "to keep you waiting so. But the fact is I got asleep; and when you knocked I awoke all in a daze, and for a minute it didn't come to me who it must be. Take the bags right upstairs, Isaphiny; and put them in the keeping-room chamber. How's your papa, Elsie—and Katy? Not laid up again, I hope?"

"Oh, no! She seems to get better all the time."

"That's right," responded Mrs. Worrett heartily. "I didn't know but what, with hot weather, and company in the house, and all—there's a chicken, Johnnie," she exclaimed, suddenly interrupting herself, as a long-legged hen ran past the door. "Want to chase it just now? You can, if you like. Or would you rather go upstairs first?"

"Upstairs, please," replied John; while Elsie went to

the door, and watched Alexander driving away down the dusty road. She felt as if their last friend had deserted them. Then she and Johnnie followed Isaphiny upstairs. Mrs. Worrett never "mounted" in hot weather, she told them.

The spare chamber was just under the roof. It was very hot, and smelt as if the windows had never been opened since the house was built. As soon as they were alone, Elsie ran across the room and threw up the sash; but the moment she let go, down it fell again with a crash which shook the floor and made the pitcher dance and rattle in the wash-bowl. The children were dreadfully frightened, especially when they heard Mrs. Worrett at the foot of the stairs calling to ask what was the matter.

"It's only the window," explained Elsie, going into the hall. "I'm so sorry; but it won't stay open. Something's the matter with it."

"Did you stick the nail in?" inquired Mrs. Worrett.

"The nail? No, ma'am."

"Why, how on earth did you expect it to stay up then? You young folks never see what's before your eyes. Look on the window-sill, and you'll find it. It's put there on purpose."

Elsie returned, much discomfited. She looked and, sure enough, there was a big nail, and there was a hole in the side of the window-frame in which to stick it. This time she got the window open without accident; but a long blue paper shade caused her much embarrassment. It hung down, and kept the air from coming in. She saw no way of fastening it.

"Roll it up, and put in a pin," suggested John.

"I'm afraid of tearing the paper. Dear, what a horrid thing it is!" replied Elsie, in a disgusted tone.

However, she stuck in a couple of pins and fastened

175

the shade out of the way. After that, they looked about the room. It was plainly furnished, but very nice and neat. The bureau was covered with a white towel, on which stood a pin-cushion, with "Remember Ruth" stuck upon it in pins. John admired this very much, and felt that she could never make up her mind to spoil the pattern by taking out a pin, however great her need of one might be.

"What a high bed!" she exclaimed. "Elsie, you'll have to climb on a chair to get into it; and so shall I."

Elsie felt of it. "Feathers!" she cried in a tone of horror. "O John! Why did we come? What shall we do?"

"I think we shan't mind it much," replied John, who was perfectly well, and considered these little variations on home habits rather as fun than otherwise. But Elsie gave a groan. Two nights on a feather-bed! How should she bear it!

Tea was ready in the kitchen when they went downstairs. A small fire had been lighted to boil the water. It was almost out, but the room felt stiflingly warm, and the butter was so nearly melted that Mrs. Worrett had to help it with a teaspoon. Buzzing flies hovered above the table, and gathered thick on the plate of cake. The bread was excellent, and so were the cottage cheeses and the stewed quince; but Elsie could eat nothing. She was in a fever of heat. Mrs. Worrett was distressed at this want of appetite; and so was Mr. Worrett, to whom the children had just been introduced. He was a kindly looking old man, with a bald head, who came to supper in his shirtsleeves, and was as thin as his wife was fat.

"I'm afraid the little girl don't like her supper, Lucinda," he said. "You must see about getting her something different tomorrow."

"Oh, it isn't that! Everything is very nice, only I'm not hungry," pleaded Elsie, feeling as if she should like to cry. She did cry a little after tea, as they sat in the dusk; Mr. Worrett smoking his pipe and slapping mosquitoes outside the door, and Mrs. Worrett sleeping rather noisily in a big rocking-chair. But not even Johnnie found out that she was crying; for Elsie felt that she was the naughtiest child in the world to behave so badly when everybody was so kind to her. She repeated this to herself many times, but it didn't do much good. As often as the thought of home and Katy and Papa came, a wild longing to get back to them would rush over her, and her eyes would fill again with sudden tears.

The night was very uncomfortable. Not a breath of wind was stirring, or none found its way to the stifling bed where the little sisters lay. John slept pretty well, in spite of heat and mosquitoes, but Elsie hardly closed her eyes. Once she got up and went to the window, but the blue paper shade had become unfastened, and rattled down upon her head with a sudden bump, which startled her very much. She could find no pins in the dark, so she left it hanging; whereupon it rustled and flapped through the rest of the night, and did its share towards keeping her awake. About three o'clock she fell into a doze; and it seemed only a minute after that before she awoke to find bright sunshine in the room, and half a dozen roosters crowing and calling under the windows. Her head ached violently. She longed to stay in bed, but was afraid it would be thought impolite: so she dressed and went down with Johnnie; but she looked so pale and ate so little breakfast that Mrs. Worret was quite troubled, and said she had better not try to go out, but just lie on the lounge in the best room, and amuse herself with a book.

The lounge in the best room was covered with slippery, purple chintz. It was a high lounge and very narrow. There was nothing at the end to hold the pillow in its place; so the pillow constantly tumbled off and jerked Elsie's head suddenly backward, which was not at all comfortable. Worse— Elsie having dropped into a doze, she herself tumbled to the floor, rolling from the glassy, smooth chintz as if it had been a slope of ice. This adventure made her so nervous that she dared not go to sleep again, though Johnnie fetched two chairs, and placed them beside the sofa to hold her on. So she followed Mrs. Worrett's advice, and "amused herself with a book". There were not many books in the best room. The one Elsie chose was a fat black volume called *The Complete Works of Mrs. Hannah More*. Part of it was prose, and part was poetry. Elsie began with a chapter called "Hints on the Formation of the Character of a Youthful Princess". But there were a great many long words in it; so she turned to a story named "Cœlebs in Search of a Wife". It was about a young gentleman who wanted to get married, but who didn't feel sure that there were any young ladies nice enough for him; so he went about making visits, first to one and then to another; and, when he had stayed a few days at a house, he would always say, "No, she won't do," and then he would go away. At last he found a young lady who seemed the very person, who visited the poor, and got up early in the morning, and always wore white, and never forgot to wind up her watch or do her duty; and Elsie almost thought that now the difficult young gentleman must be satisfied, and say, "This is the very thing." When, lo! her attention wandered a little, and the next thing she knew she was rolling off the lounge for the second time, in company with Mrs. Hannah More. They landed in the chairs, and Johnnie ran and picked them both up. Altogether, lying on the best parlour sofa was not very restful; and as the day went on, and the sun beating on the blindless windows made the room hotter, Elsie grew continually more and more feverish and homesick and disconsolate.

Meanwhile Johnnie was kept in occupation by Mrs. Worret, who had got the idea firmly fixed in her mind that the chief joy of a child's life was to chase chickens. Whenever a hen fluttered past the kitchen door, which was about once in three minutes, she would cry: "Here, Johnnie, here's another chicken for you to chase," and poor Johnnie would feel obliged to dash out into the sun. Being a very polite little girl, she did not like to say to Mrs. Worrett that running in the heat was disagreeable: so by dinner time she was thoroughly tired, and would have been cross if she had known how; but she didn't—Johnnie was never cross. After dinner it was even worse; for the sun was hotter, and the chickens, who didn't mind sun, seemed to be walking all the time. "Hurry, Johnnie, here's another," came so constantly, that at last Elsie grew desperate, got up, and went to the kitchen with a languid appeal: "Please, Mrs. Worrett, won't you let Johnnie stay by me, because my head aches so hard?" After that Johnnie had rest; for Mrs.Worrett was the kindest of women, and had no idea that she was not amusing her little guest in the most delightful manner.

A little before six, Elsie's head felt better; and she and Johnnie put on their hats, and went for a walk in the garden. There was not much to see: beds of vegetables—a few currant bushes—that was all. Elsie was leaning against a paling, and trying to make out why the Worrett house had that queer tiptoe expression, when a sudden loud grunt startled her, and something

179

touched the top of her head. She turned, and there was an enormous pig, standing on his hind legs, on the other side of the paling. He was taller than Elsie, as he stood thus, and it was his cold nose which had touched her head. Somehow, appearing in this unexpected way, he seemed to the children like some dreadful wild beast. They screamed with fright and fled to the house, from which Elsie never ventured to stir again during their visit. John chased the chickens at intervals, but it was a doubtful pleasure; and all the time she kept a wary eye on the distant pig.

That evening, while Mrs. Worrett slept and Mr. Worrett smoked outside the door, Elsie felt so very miserable that she broke down altogether. She put her head in Johnnie's lap, as they sat together in the darkest corner of the room, and sobbed and cried, making as little noise as she possibly could. Johnnie comforted her with soft pats and strokings; but did not dare to say a word, for fear Mrs. Worrett should wake up and find them out.

When morning came, Elsie's one thought was, Would Alexander come for them in the afternoon? All day she watched the clock and the road with feverish anxiety. Oh! if Papa had changed his mind—had decided to let them stay for a week at Conic Section—what would she do? It was just possible to worry through and keep alive till afternoon, she thought; but if they were forced to spend another night in that feather-bed, with these mosquitoes, hearing the blue shade rattle and quiver hour after hour—she should die, she was sure she should die!

But Elsie was not called upon to die, or even to discover how easy it is to survive a little discomfort. About five, her anxious watch was rewarded by the appearance of a cloud of dust, out of which presently emerged old Whitey's ears and the top of the well-known carriage. They stopped at the gate. There was Alexander, brisk and smiling, very glad to see his "little misses" again, and to find them so glad to go home. Mrs. Worrett, however, did not discover that they were glad; no indeed! Elsie and John were much too polite for that. They thanked the old lady, and said goodbye so prettily that, after they were gone, she told Mr. Worrett that it hadn't been a bit of trouble having them there, and she hoped they would come again; they enjoyed everything so much; only it was a pity that Elsie looked so peaked. And at that very moment Elsie was sitting on the floor of the carriage, with her head in John's lap, crying and sobbing for joy that the visit was over, and that she was on the way home. "If only I live to get there," she said, "I'll never, no, never, go into the country again!" Which was silly enough; but we must forgive her because she was not very well.

Ah, how charming home did look, with the family grouped in the shady porch, Katy in her white dress! Clover with rosebuds in her belt, and everybody ready to welcome and pet the little absentees! There was much hugging and kissing, and much to tell of what had happened in the two days: how a letter had come from Cousin Helen; how Daisy White had four kittens as white as herself; how Dorry had finished his water-wheel—a wheel which turned in the bathtub, and was "really ingenious", Papa said; and Phil had "swapped" one of his bantam chicks for one of Eugene Slack's Brahmapootras.

It was not till they were all seated round the tea-table that anybody demanded an account of the visit. Elsie felt this a relief, and was just thinking how delicious everything was, from the sliced peaches to the clinking ice in the milk-pitcher, when Papa put the dreaded question:

"Well, Elsie, so you decided to come, after all. How was it? Why didn't you stay your week out? You look pale, it seems to me. Have you been enjoying yourself too much? Tell us all about it."

Elsie looked at Papa, and Papa looked at Elsie. Dr. Carr's eyes twinkled just a little, but otherwise he was perfectly grave. Elsie began to speak, then to laugh, then to cry, and the explanation, when it came, was given in a mingled burst of all three.

"O Papa, it was horrid! That is, Mrs. Worrett was just as kind as could be, but so fat; and oh, such a pig! I never imagined such a pig. And the calico on that horrid sofa was so slippery that I rolled off five times, and once I hurt myself very badly. And we had a feather-bed; and I was so homesick that I cried all the evening."

"That must have been gratifying to Mrs. Worrett," put in Dr. Carr.

"Oh, she didn't know it, Papa. She was asleep, and snoring so that nobody could hear. And the flies!—such flies, Katy!—and the mosquitoes, and our window wouldn't open till I put in a nail. I am so glad to get home! I never want to go into the country again, never, never! Oh, if Alexander hadn't come!—why, Clover, what are you laughing for? And Dorry—I think it's very unkind," and Elsie ran to Katy, hid her face, and began to cry.

"Never mind, darling, they didn't mean to be unkind. Papa, her hands are quite hot; you must give her something." Katy's voice shook a little; but she would not hurt Elsie's feelings by showing that she was amused. Papa gave Elsie "something" before she went to bed—a very mild dose, I fancy; for doctors' little girls, as a general rule, do not take medicine; and next day she was much better. As the adventures of the

182

Conic Section visit leaked out bit by bit, the family laughed till it seemed as if they would never stop. Phil was for ever enacting the pig, standing on his triumphant hind legs, and patting Elsie's head with his nose; and many and many a time, "It will end like your visit to Mrs. Worrett," proved a useful check when Elsie was in a self-willed mood and bent on some scheme which for the moment struck her as delightful. For one of the good things about our childish mistakes is, that each one teaches us something; and so, blundering on, we grow wiser, till, when the time comes, we are ready to take our place among the wonderful grown-up people who never make mistakes.